Liberated

Presents:

REALITY
CHECK
REASON

LiberatedPublishing.com

Liberated Publishing, Inc.
1860 Wilma Rudolph Blvd
Clarksville, TN 37040

Copyright © 2010 Richard "Reason" Garrett

Published by: Liberated Publishing, Inc.

ISBN: 978-0-982552346

First Printing: December 2010

Printed in the United States of America

This book could be dedicated to so many different individuals for their support that the acknowledgements alone could be a short story. So I would like to thank everyone who has been inspirational in their own way of encouraging me to complete <u>Reality Check</u>.

Of course I would also like to thank those who may have harbored ill will in their attempts to deter me from my vision. You all served as motivation and fuel for me to overcome all obstacles.

Last, but certainly not least, I would like to thank God. Had it not been for His grace and mercy, I can only speculate where I would be.

Prologue

Clarksville, Tennessee, better known these days as Clarksvegas as it becomes more and more of a gamble to hustle in these once quiet streets. With another high crime rate summer coming to a close, I find myself caught up in the aftermath of what should have been another clockwork home invasion.

"Mr. Williamson… Mr. Williamson turn to the right please," barked the sour faced butch looking deputy.

As Tavares, also known as Tee, slowly complied, her frustration and impatience becomes more evident in her voice. "You low lifes may have nothing but time on your hands, but I on the other hand don't." With an indignant stare she continued, "Now place your thumb here and roll it when I tell you."

Once the fingerprinting was completed, Tavares was escorted back to the bullpen to await his phone call and finish processing. Quickly scanning the room for a place to sit, he counted at least seven other "low lifes", all ranging in ages between 17 and 45. There were two blacks, two whites, two Hispanics, and a Korean. The women's bullpen appeared to house the same type of melting pot mix, so he reasoned with himself that it was safe to assume that "low life" was meant as an equal opportunity dis rather than a prejudiced one. Not that it mattered much considering it wouldn't have been the first racist comments that he'd put up with from insecure spiteful deputies. Just the mere thought of them brought back memories that were all too real for him.

It had begun on a Saturday night, October 27, 2002 to be exact. The crew had thrown Tavares a party to celebrate his long awaited 18th birthday. With this event also signifying his early retirement from hustling and a new beginning they planned to make it a night to be remembered. The bar at Club Reasons was stocked with more alcohol than your average liquor store, with DJ Butterfly spinning nothing but hits. It appeared that Clarksville's finest were dressed to impress as they dominated the dance floor.

As the crew made their way past the bar to the VIP lounge, they caught the attention of some of the envious hustlers from around the way. Upon entering the veiled lounge, they were greeted by one of the three topless waitresses serving the lounge.

"Hi, my name is Sasha and I'll be your hostess tonight," she said as she made eye contact with each member of the clique then settling on Tavares before she continued, "tonight your wish is my command," with a seductive wink.

"For starters you can bring us four bottles of Kristal," he replied as his eyes took in her vivacious frame.

"Let me show you to your seats and I'll be right back with your drinks," she said as she pivoted and began to sashay towards one of the tables in the back corner.

"Dang nigga, you see the onion booty on that freak!" Chris exclaimed.

"How could you miss that ignorant tail? It's almost colliding into everything she walks past," Donovan joked.

"Yeah, I bet she could balance our drinks along with a full course meal on all that," Roe added.

After seating the group, Sasha sauntered off to fetch the drinks leaving Chris in a trance as his eyes watched Sasha's hips sway like a pendulum.

"Earth to Captain Kirk... I repeat Earth to Captain Kirk," Donovan said.

"Snap out of it fam and put your tongue back in ya mouth," Roe added.

"Forget you mane ain't nobody stuntin' her," Chris retorted.

"Let you tell it," Tee added.

Just as Chris was about to put his foot in his

mouth, Sasha returned with their drinks.

"Anything else I can do for you gentleman?" Sasha asked.

"Yeah, do you make house calls?" Chris asked as his eyes became infatuated with her ripe nipples.

Already knowing who was who in the group she sized him up and replied, "I doubt you could afford the bill," as she walked off.

"Screw you, you old sadiddy ho!" he exploded.

"Chill, tonight ain't even the night for all that drama."

"Plus there's way too many where she came from out there," Donovan said, pointing to the dance floor that they could see through the one- way mirror.

"Now if you're done being sensitive I'd like to propose a toast." Raising his bottle, Tee continued, "To new beginnings!"

"To new beginnings!" they all replied as they toasted.

After the fourth round of drinks Tavares could feel the alcohol running through his system so he excused himself and headed for the restroom.

Unbeknown to him, his movements were being clocked as he maneuvered his way through the crowd and entered the men's room.

Dee, having seen his opportunity, eased his gloves on before trailing after Tavares. Reaching the door, he withdrew a .45 and entered.

As Tavares was finishing up his business, Dee made his move, "Come up off that cash fool!"

Before Tavares could even react, the barrel was firmly planted against his temple.

"Mane you slippin' big time these days."

"Maybe, but you would have never lived to talk about it."

"How soooooooo?"

Just then Tony bursts in with his .9 drawn.

"We strait fam," Tee said.

Tony acknowledged him and went back to his post. As they dapped each other up, Tee sized his former coworker up. It had been a little over a year since they had done that last robbery together. "I've been meaning to get at you fam."

"Nigga stop playing. You already know what it is."

"Yeah, I dig how you trying to rise above the nonsense and do the family man thing." Clearing his throat, he continued, *"I'm trying to get myself together so I can get on that real estate hustle too."*

"Like they say, knowledge is power. Pick up a few books and read up on it."

"I never was one to read instructions. How about we take this back to the VIP lounge and discuss this over some of this purp," he said as he removed an ounce from a crown royal bag concealed in his crotch and handed it to him.

"Mmm, haze never stank so good," Tee said while taking a whiff the pungent odor.

"And it smokes that much better," Dee said, trying to seal the deal.

"I don't mind matching one wit ya, but we gon have to reschedule that knowledge session."

"Bet," Dee said, taking the bag back then following Tavares as he led the way back to the lounge.

As they approached the veiled entrance, Tee waived off the security guard enroute to check Dee's

6

credentials. Once inside they joined the rest of the crew, who already had two blunts in rotation.

Midway into the session Sasha returned to check on her potential meal ticket for the evening. Although she knew through the grapevine that the "wifey" had him on lock, she lived by the motto, "Nothing ventured, nothing gained," as she continued her routine of leaning in as close to Tee as possible, where her protruding chocolate mounds dangled in front of him like ripe cherries. Setting the drink before him, she leaned in close enough for her lips to touch his ear and said, "It's from the sadiddy ho. She also wanted to make sure you knew that she meant every bit of granting your most erotic wish tonight."

Almost on cue, Ariana entered the lounge accompanied by Lashay and Brittany.

"See gurl, I told you her skank behind was gonna be working the VIP tonight." Brittany said.

"Yeah, she's definitely working a V.I.P. tonight," Lashay said, adding fuel to the fire.

"Naw, what this ho is really working on is getting her tail kicked all through this lounge," Ariana said as she led the charge. Just before Ariana reached Sasha, security hurriedly intervened, stepping between the two. Knowing better than to lay a hand on Ariana, they grabbed Sasha and escorted her out of the lounge.

As the altercation died down, Ariana calmly strolled where her lips skimmed his earlobe and whispered, "I just wanted to wish you a happy birthday and remind you of what you got waiting at home," she said, nibbling on his lobe and allowing her tongue to tickle the crease behind his ear. Lustful thoughts began to fill his mind as he reveled in the ecstasy that these images conjured up.

Content in knowing her message was received, she withdrew and signaled to her friends who were mingling with the rest of the crew, that it was time to depart.

As the girls sauntered away out of earshot, Donovan began to brag about how he had Lashay practically dripping soak and wet on his lap.

"When it's all said and done I might have to tuck shawty in tonight," he continued.

"What we need to do is hit the floor and jump on some of them boppers out there," Roe commented.

"I'm wit that. I seen this fly Thai and Vietnamese chic clocking me from the moment my J's touched down on the red carpet," Donovan boasted.

"How the hell you gon pick out a mix like that?" Chris inquired.

"Cuz a play boi like me do his homework junior."

8

As the duo traded banters, Dee noticed Tee seemed restless. It was common knowledge in the streets that Tavares wasn't into the whole club scene. He'd much rather throw get togethers at his jump off spot where the only expectations were getting blunted and kicking it with people he was cool with. Having done his own homework, he knew that although Tee had quite a few rides, he hardly ever drove anywhere. With the rest of the crew hyped up about the party he would spoil the evening for his crew if he wanted to leave early.

"This scene is starting to kill my buzz." When Tee didn't bite, he continued, "Say fam, I'm fend to make moves, you trying to dip?"

Weighing his options, Tee figured he could get Dee to drop him off in the subdivision across from his and hoof it to the crib.

"Might as well. Ain't nothing out here except the same old hype."

After the farewells were exchanged, they made use of the side exit with Dee leading the way.

As they approached his whip, Tavares had to give Dee his props. Just a year ago, he was riding around in a tired looking Gallant. Now look at him. The 2010 Cadillac Supercharger was a definite upgrade with its cherry red exterior, peanut butter leather seats, along with the 24" Giovanni rims gave it the edge it needed to

9

turn heads.

"You wanna hit a few blocks?" Peeping his reluctance he added, "I already know your getaway driving side wanna at least punch it a couple times."

Against his better judgment, Tee gave in and took the keys. As they traveled down Riverside Dr. doing barely three over the speed limit, Tavares noticed that two more cars and a van joined the beige Acura Legend that had been following for the past ten minutes. Sensing something awry, he glanced at Dee, who either had no clue of what was happening or was doing a good job of pretending. Scanning ahead, he saw the light change yellow. Adjusting his speed, he then crossed the intersection just as the light turned red, with his pursuers gaining on him as they ran the light.

"We've got company."

"It appears so.... Make this next right," he said coolly.

Almost as soon as Tavares turned on Robb Ave., he ran into a roadblock, with the trailing vehicles coming to a screeching halt, boxing him in followed by vice exploding from their cars with weapons drawn.

As Tee's mind began to frantically put together what was going down, Dee casually exited the vehicle and walked past the officers into the night.

10

For the Clarksville Police Department, it was an open and shut case. The Leaf Chronicle would go on to describe how an officer pulled Tavares Williamson over in a stolen Cadillac with a little over a Big 8 of soft and a .45 with the serial numbers scratched off.

"Mr. Williamson!" the guard called out, bringing him back to reality. As the door opened he continued, "Come with me please." After the door was secured, he was given the opportunity to place a phone call.

"Hello?"

"I got a situation."

"What's going on son?"

"I can't get into it right now. Call Ariana and get her to calm down and explain everything to you. I'll call again later on in the week once I have more info for you."

"I don't like the sound of this one bit. You said you were through with that foolishness."

"Dad, now ain't the time to get into all that. Just get up with Ariana and make sure she's taken care of."

"Alright son. We're here for you and will be praying for you. Just make sure you keep us informed."

"Will do."

As the line went dead, Tavares could not help but think how he had let his family down again. They had such high expectations that his last extended vacation had been enough of a wakeup call for the prodigal son to truly come home.

Chapter 1

One week later…

"Hey gurl, you trying to hit up the Rivergate Mall and try out that new Jamaican restaurant in Nashville?" Lashay said, trying to get Ariana's mind off Tee.

"Naw, I'm cool. Somebody's gotta hold down the fort."

"Gurl, that's what he got HPC out there for. You know that hit squad be reckin' shop in the streets."

"Forget the streets. The streets are what keep taking him from me. This is about home."

"Well, if ya need me you know how to reach me," Lashay said, as she went to let herself out.

Once Ariana heard the lock click she allowed the tears to stream down her face as feelings of anger, frustration, and anxiety began to rage against her already unstable hormones causing her mind to drift…

It was a morning like any other with the exception that she was up before 12:00 pm on a weekend. She had her suspicions even after just taking one a week ago with the results coming back negative.

13

So here she finds herself taking yet another test as she brings up the little stick that would put all her fears to ease. At least she hoped so, especially after last week's scare when Tee decided to put on an Oscar winning performance as if he were about to be the world's happiest father to be.

After finishing and placing the stick on the sink, she went into the kitchen for a glass of water, and then lit a cigarette as she waited on the results.

Meanwhile Tavares was still passed out from last night's get together.

Unable to take the anticipation she stubbed out the half smoked New Port and went to check the results.

"Pregnant... Why me?" she cried out in total disbelief as if her vision must have been blurred.

"Let me wake this nigga up and see if it's just too early in the morning and I'm delusional," she said.

Entering the room, her arm began trembling uncontrollably as she approached the bed with the stick palmed tightly in her hand.

Tee, on the other hand, unaware of the pending news, began wiping the crust from his eyes as her trembling frame came into view.

14

"Baby... baby what is it?" he asks groggily.

"Read this," she simply said while passing the test to Tavares, who accepted it with a smirk on his face as if this were pay back for last week's prank when he started jumping up and down while shouting, "I'm gonna be a daddy, I'm gonna be a daddy!"

Almost immediately, that smug expression turned into one that she couldn't quite discern. Before she could prompt a response out of him, Tee slowly pulled her in close and whispered, "Baby, I'm gonna do what I gotta do to take care of us."

Unable to speak, she wrapped her arms snugly around him and began to think back to when they had made love and he started talking foolishly about going half on a baby. Hell, with the way he was working it, she would have been liable to agree to anything at the moment.

The ringing telephone broke her trance. "Hello."

"You have a collect phone call from....Tee....an inmate in the Clarksville Montgomery County Jail. To acce"—(Beep).

"Hey baby, did you get the books and 24 hour bag?"

"Yea, I got it. It means a lot that you're out there

holding me down."

"It would mean a lot more if you were here holding me."

"This ain't like last time baby. They got me in here over a whole lot of nothing right now. Even Clarksville's worst public defender couldn't mess this case up."

"The point is, it shouldn't be like any time," Ariana retorted.

"Look, I'd rather not spend this hot 10 minutes bickering and carrying on. I gotta hurry up and get back to the house to tie up a few loose ends." Tee paused to allow that to sink in before continuing; "Now I need you to go ahead and clean up the spot and get Donovan to help you. Then let pops know my next hearing is…"

"You're a little late on all that baby. The house is spotless and I've already been in touch with your lawyer and dad. We all gonna be at your hearing next week."

"What the fam up to?"

"Depends on who you calling fam these days." As Tee's brows arched into a questioning look, she continued, "You already know I went through your phone calling niggaz like a telemarketer. And for the most part fam represented."

"The most part huh?"

"Baby I know you grew up with a lot of these cats, but you really need to drop all these fake dudes out here fronting like they G's."

"How are things sounding on the outside?"

"Quiet for now."

"As long as it stays that way, I'll address the issue in due time. Till then my main focus is getting things back on track."

"And which track would that be?"

"You already know."

"I can't tell. These days you're out there more than you're at home."

"Now that it's more than just me and you, I gots to be a provider first. This right here ain't nothing but a minor setback that we'll overcome together, and then move forward from."

"I really do hope so Tee. I love the hell out of you but"—
(Beep), "You have ten seconds remaining."

"Well there you have it then. There is no time for

17

buts. Only forward progress. Ariana, always know my heart is forever yours."

"As mine is yours…" (Beep)

As the call abruptly ended, the harsh reality of his surroundings came into focus. Granted, H pod was a lot better than G, where he was locked down for 23 straight. Plus having a connected cellie was an added bonus.

Anything Tee needed, from books to commissary, was at his disposal. Deciding to stretch his legs a bit, Tee began his usual route around the pod passing groups, playing spades, and working out.

The buzzing noise from the cell doors being unlocked signaled the end of rec call for the evening. By the time he made it to the second level and entered his cell, Byrd was already settled in on his rack reading a copy of Sensual Delights.

"You trying to get at some of these cookies fam?" Byrd said holding out a pack of vanilla wafers. "I won 3 packs from them chumps in 11."

"Yeah, I'll hit up a couple," Tee replied.

"Go head and take the whole thing. I got two extra breakfast trays coming in the morning."

"What we having?"

"Boiled eggs and gravy."

"I'm good on that gravy. Last time it did a number on my stomach."

"Everything straight on the home front?"

"Looks that way. If half of what my lawyer says is true, I'll be out of here by next week."

"I figured as much. So what you gonna get into first once you hit the streets?"

"Other than taking care of home, then hitting up moms fridge, I plan on keeping a low profile for a few months."

"That's probably your best bet. I don't even know the whole story and don't want to, but from the sound of things you already know them boys gonna be watching."

"All I need is about 3 to 4 years, and then they can watch all they want."

"Got a show planned do we?"

"More like a vision that will become a reality."

"I'm listening."

"After being inspired by Vickie Stringer's novel, Let That Be The Reason while serving four years, I

19

began researching a bunch of legit hustles with the goal of building a self-sufficient real estate empire."

"You going it alone or with partners?"

"Eventually I'm gonna need help with it, but for now I'm straight with it just being me. For some reason our people haven't learned from some of the other races. Instead of networking together to accomplish something, people would rather act like a bunch of crabs in a bucket."

"Pulling down the next person trying to climb out."

"Exactly."

"Good luck wit all that fam," Byrd said as he went back to reading Sensual Delights. With only about an hour left before the lights went out, Tee climbed up to his bunk and drifted off to sleep.

Chapter 2

The following afternoon Ariana found herself flipping through the scrapbook she had recently put together when Tee's phone began to ring. Figuring it was just HPC checking up on her she didn't bother answering.

Later that evening as she entered the bedroom, she heard Tee's voice mail tone going off and decided to be nosy.

"You have two unheard messages... Press one to— (Beep)"

"What's really good fam. This Donovan get at me"— (Beep)

"Message deleted. Next message..."

"Ariana, this is Kid. Please pick up..."

The mere mention of his name caused her blood to run cold as images of him speaking to the detective just before Tee was arrested played through her mind. He even had the audacity to show up at Peachers Mill Hollow the day after the incident with two bodyguards just to give him the opportunity to tell his side of the story. But when it was all said and done they ended up beating the breaks off him so bad that he had to run to the apartment next door and literally throw himself at

Tina's mercy. Later that evening Tina would go on to share how Kid nearly broke down her door with his frantic pounding and wailing. As soon as she opened the door to see what the entire racket was about, he flung his body inside on the carpet then began flailing his legs about trying to quickly close the door behind him.

"...I can understand that you don't want to speak to me, but I'm desperate. I can't even go to work without HPC waiting for me in the parking lot. You have to do something, please. I didn't mean it. I didn't mean to"—

(Beep). "Message deleted. You have no more messages remaining. Good-bye."

Disgusted, Ariana placed the phone back on the nightstand. Grabbing the keys, she locked up and went to visit her friend Brittany.

{{{{{{{{{{{{{{{}}}}}}}}}}}}}}}

Meanwhile in Metropolis, Illinois, Donovan, having wrapped business up early and checked on Ariana, decided to spend the evening at the Harrah Casino.

From the moment Donovan entered the lobby, he caught the attention of a hostess. After a brief pause to examine her slender yet sensual frame partnered with a beautiful smile, he casually made his way across the marble floor to where she was standing beneath the chandelier. As he approached, he took notice of her arched eyebrows over tight eyes, thick eyelashes, with full lips that gave her an exotic appeal.

"Welcome to Harrah's. Is there anything I can do to make your visit more pleasant?"

"I can think of quite a few things..." Donovan said cutting his eyes towards the hotel side of the casino before settling back on hers.

"But for now I'm due for a change of luck on these tables. Care to join me for an evening meant for Vegas?"

"Only if it stays in Vegas," she replied as she hooked her arm around his and led him across the bridge onto the river boat casino.

{{{{{{{{{{{{{{{}}}}}}}}}}}}}}}

As the sun glared brightly through the Victorian windows, Donovan awoke to find his companion gone. Ordinarily this sort of thing wouldn't have fazed him a bit, but this time was different.

Although it had been one of his worse gambling nights all week in addition to him waking up with blue balls, it still beat any evening Vegas had to offer.

In all his years Donovan had never enjoyed himself more with someone as he had that night. Everything about her seemed to hold his interest, especially her intellect and fun loving nature.

As he reached for his stash of weed, he noticed a note resting on the nightstand. Picking it up, he couldn't help but smile as he read its contents.

Donovan,

I would like to thank you for being such a perfect gentleman throughout a wonderful evening. However, I do have a confession to make. Ever since Tavares' birthday party, I've been hoping our paths would cross again. I heard from a friend of mine who really works here that you frequent the casino often so I decided to pose as a hostess for the evening. I must admit with your lady's man reputation, I had my doubts. I'm glad though that I didn't let that stop me from getting to know you."

Naomi

Chapter 3

County Jail

As Tavares lay on his rack reading <u>Dutch</u> by Teri Woods, his mind began to wander back to his own trial...

"Your Honor, at this time Mr. Williamson would like to make an unsworn statement on his behalf." His attorney spoke, and then slightly nodded in his direction before sitting down.

As Tavares rose to address the courtroom, he could swear his heart was beating louder than a marching band. Having turned down the deal offered for 60 months, the prosecution had just finished summing Tavares' character as being a threat to society and deserving no less than 8 years.

"Good morning Your Honor. For the past week I have been trying to decide how to begin this and what I could say to you about my childhood that could possibly influence you to show compassion on me in regards to my sentence. However, after putting a lot of thought and prayer into it, I decided to speak to you from the heart. I'm not here to make excuses for anything. I believe that in this instance I am about to reap the consequences of past actions,"

"Sir, for as long as I can remember, I've been caught up on trying to make it on my own. Although I

25

was born and raised in the church as a preacher's kid and knew God was real, I didn't think I needed Him in my life to make it. I took pride in being able to work out all my problems and handle business on my own. They say pride comes before the fall; well that statement definitely sums up what happened to me."

"One positive thing that I can say about these 7 months of waiting to come stand before you is that it has been time not wasted. One important lesson learned was the power of praising God, not just for the good things that happens in our lives, but also for the bad. God can use what the devil intended to bring about evil in our lives to bring about good. Just like the Prodigal Son, sometimes it takes hitting rock bottom to finally look up and see just how far you have fallen."

"Your Honor, don't get me wrong. I wouldn't mind getting out of here as soon as possible to have the opportunity to demonstrate that I can be a positive influence in our community. But at the same time, I realize that God knows what's best for me and my family and won't give us more than we can handle. I also realize that a heavy burden rests on my shoulders to redeem myself. Not only in the eyes of God, but also in the eyes of my family, who have loved and supported me unconditionally. I found out the hard way that it is not only the inmate that does the time, but also those who love and care for them because a piece of them is locked away as well."

"Your Honor, before I close, I would like to read a poem that I feel sums up my unsworn statement;"

"Trapped in a game where there is no clear winner
Which only has two paths to take, that of the righteous and that of the sinner
With principalities waging war at every fork in the road
As my eyes scan each path for the shorter route to the goal
But finding out too late that taking the easy way out has put my life on hold.
What happened to all those friends who said they'd always be there?
Turns out the family you ran from were the only ones who cared
The money, cars, girls, and crib all gone in the blink of an eye
Leaving you worse than what you started with and all you can do is wonder how and why
But deep down knowing the truth of how things turned out this way
With nothing else to do or say
Your only choice being to give it up to God and pray
For His grace and mercy to make it another day."

"Your Honor, at this time I would like to thank you for taking my statement into consideration prior to sentencing."

Rising to Tavares' side, his attorney spoke, "Your Honor, the defense has no other evidence to present at this time."

"Tavares Williamson!" barked the guard as he unlocked his cell. "You have a legal visit."

Shaking off the remnants of his trial, he followed the guard to the visitation booth and awaited his lawyer to appear on the monitor.

After what seemed like twenty minutes, the monitor came to life. Placing the receiver to his ear, Tavares braced himself for the worst.

"Good afternoon Mr. Williamson. I hope they are treating you okay in there," she said with false sincerity.

"Well it ain't nothing like a Holiday Inn, but I'll live. Do you have good news or do I need to change my mailing address?"

"From the looks of things, Thomas Berry has retracted his statement and will not be testifying. And with Quentin Smith refusing to file a complaint, the charges will be deferred for 4 to 6 months then dropped."

"Deferred? No evidence, no witnesses. Why not just dropped all together? What do you mean by deferred anyway?"

"For some reason the DA, as well as the lead detectives, have a strong suspicion that there is more to this case than any of you are willing to speak on. By deferring the charges they can hold it over your head and use it against you in addition to whatever charges they may have against you for up to 6 months."

"I ain't messed up with it. Is my date still the same?"

"Yes, it's still set for the December 5th at 10 a.m. You will more than likely be released sometime after 6 p.m. Any other questions?"

"No, that's it."

"Well, I'll see you Tuesday," she said, then placed the receiver back on the cradle and cued for the guard to kill the monitor.

Once back in the cell Tee began to plot his next move. For the next 6 months, he would have to walk on eggshells compared to the "Get Money" lifestyle that Lil Yola songs pumped through his veins.

Seeing his cellie in deep thought Byrd asked, "What's got your forehead all wrinkled up like a uni-brow?"

"Just plotting to take over the city one hustle at a time."

"So I take it things went smooth with your

lawyer?"

"Yeah things are looking up on that tip. Right now my main focus is organizing this movement."

"What you got worked out so far?"

"Just the basics for the company's structure. Haven't broke down all the departments yet, but I do know there will be a graphics design department, distribution team, as well as promotions department."

"What products you pushing?"

"Anything legit we can get our hands on and distribute for profit."

"I'm feeling that there are a lot of possibilities for a company with a large business scope. Just make sure you don't stretch yourself too thin."

"Yeah, it's gonna be tough initially, but no one is just gonna hand me the money. I need to hit the real estate market hard. So I'm gonna be grinding until I get my clean money long enough."

"Rome wasn't built in a day."

"That may be, but I intend to grind as if it were built in a month."

As the conversation wound down the two settled back into their routines of passing the time.

Chapter 4

The Spot

With the exception of small talk, the only thing filling the airwaves was the growing cloud of haze as the crew waited on Roe to arrive.

Just as Chris was about to call him for the 2nd time, they heard Roe's '77 Cutlass pull up with his system loud enough to wake the dead.

A few moments after the engine died, Roe knocked twice and was admitted by Tony.

Upon entering the room greetings were exchanged as Roe jumped into the rotation.

Taking charge Donovan addressed the crew, "Now that we're all settled in, it's time to get down to business." After a brief pause he continued, "As you all are aware, there is a lot of tension in the streets from this beef between the North and South side."

"What's that got to do with us?" Chris asked.

"I see you still wearing your helmet from the lil bus," Roe reprimanded, then explained, "With them Slab and Greenwood niggaz trying to strong arm the North you already know my Burchwood niggaz ain't going for that."

"Which is why the city done increased its police presence on the North. Now do I need to spell out why that would be bad for business?" Donovan said as he glanced directly at Chris. Taking his silence as an answer he continued, "Now given the present situation I propose we take it easy till things blow over."

"Take it easy? When has that ever been the way Hollow Point Click got down?" Roe asked.

"I ain't talking about stopping all together. We just need to cut down on the number of doors we kick in," Donovan clarified.

"You crazy. I ain't fend to let a bunch of bottom feeders mess up my flow. I'm a strait get money nigga to the fullest!" Roe exclaimed.

"I'm with Donovan on this one. Roe you seen firsthand from what happened to Tee how all this heat can affect us," Chris chimed in.

"Don't get me wrong. Tee is my boy all day err day, but that's his fault for taking on that charity case for them lames without checking Kid's street cred." Roe replied.

"I'm just glad you got that charmin ass nigga to keep his mouth shut." Donovan said.

"Unwillful compliance is what I do best," Roe

gloated as he popped his collar.

"So that explains your entourage of groupies." Chris said.

"I know this Captain Save a Ho ain't talking. With the way Quanetta got you whipped I'm surprised you still know what a groupie is," Roe shot back.

"Not in this lifetime."

"Nigga please, your nose won't even pick up the fragrance of another chic when Quanetta is within a mile radius," Donovan added.

"When did this become a rerun of Girl Friends? I could have sworn we were here to talk business. So where do we go from here?" Chris asked trying to change the subject.

"Until Tee can throw his two cents in, how about we just cautiously conduct business as usual and limit the number of robberies to one a week," Donovan suggested.

"I guess I can eat off that. When is that nigga due to hit the streets?" Roe asked.

"Sometime next week."

"Any word if Kebo knows who was behind his

spot getting run through?" Chris asked

"Naw, but he's got a pot of gold for any treacherous leprechaun willing to provide him with info. With Kid out there without a shoulder to lean on, I doubt he'll be running off at the mouth," Roe said with a cruel smile lingering on his face as he stubbed out the roach.

"Now that's settled. It's been real but I got moves to make," Donovan said glancing at his watch as he began to think about his upcoming rendezvous with Naomi.

"Which trap star you caking tonight?" Roe asked.

"You know I leave them hood rats for you to add to your groupie collection." Donovan replied.

"I ain't even trying to hear that after seeing that duck clinging to your arm at Kickers the other night," Roe added.

"What you expect me to do, tell your mom she can't get at her baby daddy no more?" Donovan said as they made their way to the door.

{{{{{{{{{{{{{{{{{}}}}}}}}}}}}}}}}}

Later that evening as Ariana and Lashay exited the Great Escape Movie Theater and began to approach her car, they noticed a lone figure posted up against Ariana's hood.

Coming to a halt, "Awe hell naw!" Ariana spat as she whipped out her pepper spray.

"Now is that any way to treat an old friend?" Dee said stepping into the light.

"Seeing that you're nowhere near being a friend, I don't see how that concerns you."

"You know I was hoping that we could be civil about this," Dee said while lifting his shirt to reveal the pistol grip of his .44. As recognition etched across Ariana's face he continued, "Look, just tell your man that it would be a shame if word got out about his botched home invasion."

"What more can you want from him? He's already done 4 years behind you being a snake in the garden."

"Such venom from such a beautiful lady. To think your life could have been so much sweeter had you chosen me over Tavares."

"I'm more than happy with the way things turned out."

"Don't speak too soon, the show has just begun." Dee said with a wink as he turned and walked off toward Hunters Point.

As his silhouette blended in with the shadows, Ariana and Lashay hurriedly entered the car and sped off.

{{{{{{{{{{{{{{{}}}}}}}}}}}}}}}

On the other side of town, Chris let his engine idle after pulling up in Quanetta's driveway as he fought the butterflies fluttering in his stomach.

"How could she do this to me?" he thought aloud as his mind relived the night he found the note from Quanetta's lesbian friend.

As its contents played repeatedly in his mind, anger began to fill the void that the butterflies left. With adrenaline pumping through his veins, Chris found himself pounding at her door without realizing he left his car running.

Just before he turned to retrieve his keys, the door swung open.

"Nigga have you lost your rabid mind!?" she exclaimed.

Having come this far, Chris decided it was too late to back down. "Naw, you're the one who done lost your mind if you think you fend to put one over on me you trifling trick." Chris spat venomously.

"Trick? Nigga you got the game all messed up."

"You is really gonna play that innocent role with ya carpet munching tendencies!?"

"Don't mess around and write a check that ya tail can't cash. Now can we go inside and discuss what's got your panties in a bunch or would you rather put on a show for the rest of Brick City?" Quanetta replied coolly before she went inside and made herself comfortable on the love seat. Choosing the sofa directly across from her, Chris paused to collect himself as he fought the urge to explode again.

"Look, I know all about you and Champagne. Right now I'm past mad and into something serious. If you have something to say, then here and now is the time to say it."

"You know for someone who has never taken acting lessons you sure could be up in Hollywood."

"I ain't trying to hear anything out your mouth right now unless it's an explanation for that note I found."

"Fine, you really want the truth? Well here it is strait one hundred. I had my gurl Sasha write that note then I left it in a discreet enough spot that even your simple behind could find."

"Yeah and you expect me to buy that one?"

"I could really care less at this point. Seems like you would rather buy pussy anyway."

"What the hell are you talking about?"

"I guess you decided that on account of me always having your back even when you were at your worst, I also had boo boo the fool tattooed across my forehead." Seeing the perplexed look on his face she continued, "Remember a few weeks ago when you left your phone over here? Well I never thought twice about going through it until you acted paranoid by wanting me to cut it off and leave it off. You really should delete the pictures and text messages that those nasty hoes be sending you."

"Baby hold up, I can explain. See what had happened was..."

"Save it for someone without a clue. And to think you had the nerve to call me a trifling trick when you're the one putting them hood rats at the Cat West through medical school." Before Chris could reply she continued, "Now you already know I ain't one for drama so let's keep this as drama free as possible. Feel free to use the garbage bags under the sink to round up your belongings before I throw them out on the street."

"After all we've been through, you just gonna end

things like that?"

"You ended things a long time ago when you quit keeping it one hundred," she said as she stood up then walked into her bedroom shutting the door behind her.

Feeling defeated, Chris gathered up his things and locked the door behind him as he left.

Stepping outside, Chris peered into the night sky and wondered if things could get any worse.

Almost immediately, Murphy's Law seemed to come to pass like a Biblical prophecy as Chris noticed the empty parking space that his car once occupied.

{{{{{{{{{{{{{{{{}}}}}}}}}}}}}}}}}

After scooping Naomi up, Donovan navigated his car down Peachers Mill Rd. while "Same Differences" played in the background.

"So where are we headed?" Naomi asked.

"You'll see once we get there."

"You know I don't like surprises."

"Well you don't have to like it to love it." Feigning disappointment, Naomi pouted her bottom lip as she gazed at Donovan with puppy dog eyes.

Not buying the act, Donovan turned up the volume just as "Rain" began to play.

"I just love this song. It reminds me of the day we officially met."

Just as the track began to fade, Donovan slowed to a halt in front of an old English style brick house with cars parked bumper to bumper in the driveway wrapping around the house.

"Dang baby, what y'all got going on over here? Looks like a Kappa frat party."

"Not quite, its poker night."

"Don't you ever get tired of poker?"

"Yeah, but usually after a nap I'm ready to go again."

"You got issues," she joked.

"You don't even know the half of it. I have the pokers anonymous hotline number that the casino gives out memorized by heart."

"What would it take to kick the habit?"

"One of two things... I either cash out a million dollars richer or I get you to propose."

"Looks like we better hurry and get in there then. With goals like that every hand counts," she teased.

"I'm gonna remember that when you're giving me that I'm bored and ready to leave look."

"And miss out on something worth more than that hot million?" she asked while flirtatiously batting her lashes.

"If it's as priceless as you say then maybe I need to leave poker alone and switch back to hide and go get it," he replied just as they were admitted into the poker house.

Although it was just an apartment, from the way everything was laid out it resembled a mini casino. On the first floor the grand poker table dominated the center of the room, with two plasma screens along the walls, and a make shift bar in the corner.

After a few mediocre hands, Donovan began to grow restless and bored with his progress. "You wanna try your luck?" he asked.

"Of course," Naomi replied with a cocky grin.

The cards were dealt and to her disappointment she folded a two and a three. Skeptical of the outcome of the next hand she patiently awaited as a slender dark skinned guy with a sharp look raised the pot by $600 and won with a full house.

After the 2nd hand was dealt Naomi had pocket fours and added $500 to the pot as the small blind. The bids went around again with most of the players folding out. Sticking around for the turn to come out as queen, eight, and seven. Her other two competitors raised the bid up to $2,400. Not wanting to risk it she folded again.

Growing weary of the game, Naomi decided to play one more hand with the dealer dropping her off with pocket queens. The pot was high from the start with a small blind of $1,500 and the big blind of $3,000. Deciding to run with it, she raised the bid by $3,000.

All players folded out except for Naomi and the slender sharp competitor from earlier. The flop came out as queen, two, queen; which gave Naomi a four of a kind. She raised half of her stack with him following suit. The turn was an ace with both of them going all in.

The river was a four with her competitor confidently showing a full house with three aces only to lose the pot to her four of a kind.

Content with her winnings, Naomi leaned in close and whispered in Donovan's ear, "I'm ready to cash out and celebrate."

"Why so soon? Looks like your luck was just turning around," he replied.

"So it seems, but the true test will be pulling you away from this table so we can both get lucky," she purred as her hand slid to his lap.

"Aite ma, forget a hotline number. I've found the cure." Turning to the dealer he continued, "Hey fam, I'm done for the evening."

"You feeling okay?" he asked with a raised eyebrow.

"Nigga must be sick or something. You know that pokerholic will go for broke playing by himself."

"Either that or he's worried about going home broke," another player added.

"Naw, I just have better things to look at than y'all all night." Placing one arm around Naomi and using the other to push his chips toward the dealer he continued, "Now come up off my paper, I got moves to make."

After farewells were exchanged, the duo found themselves in deep thought as they traveled in silence.

Although Donovan would not be her first, she had been celibate for almost two years. Having come out of an emotionally abusive relationship that resulted in her being told that all she was good for was laying on her back, almost made her give up on men. Her despair went on for months until her best friend Celeste intervened

45

and persuaded her to finally get the courage to go after her secret crush.

Donovan, on the other hand, was absorbed in his own thoughts, having been threatened by Celeste not to push the issue or hurt her girl, had been patiently waiting for her to come around.

As they turned into the Pembrook Place subdivision, Donovan glanced over at her just in time to catch a single tear escape her clinched eyelids.

"You wanna talk about it?"

Wiping her face she replied, "No, I just want to get this over with."

"Get what over with?"

"I'll give you credit, you've been a gentleman so far, but in the end all it boils down to is winning the pot," she sneered.

"That's what this is about? Forget the gentleman act! You're the one who came at me like you was all about it. What you expect me to make you fill out a questionnaire to see if you're really ready to take it there."

"Don't get smart nigga. You know what, just take me home. Can you do that?"

"Gladly."

Chapter 5

One week later...

As Tavares' feet touched down on free ground, he pauses to allow the fresh night air a moment to cycle through his lungs.

Having had his cell phone confiscated as evidence, Tee had to rely on his one phone call to make arrangements for a ride home which went to voice mail after the 2nd ring.

Already knowing she was probably screening her calls, he left a message. As he crossed the street, he scanned the parking lot for any familiar vehicles. Seeing none, he enters the four story parking garage and takes the elevator to the top then walks to the ledge that overlooks the Cumberland River and straddles prior to gazing off into the horizon.

{{{{{{{{{{{{{{{{}}}}}}}}}}}}}}}}

Meanwhile, as the car slowed to a halt at the light, Ariana's mind kept racing on.

Hoping this was the last time she would be picking him up like this she thought back to his last extended stay.

Coming from a broken home where her father, an

ex-drug dealer turned drug addict, used to beat and steal from her mother until she finally had him arrested.

Struggling to rebuild their lives, her mom worked two jobs just to barely make ends meet in Ramblewood. She did her best to motivate her only child to excel in school and pick her relationships wisely so she wouldn't have to endure her hardships.

During high school in an attempt to supplement her income to be able to afford new clothes for Ariana, she went to a local plasma center to donate blood. Three weeks later they notified her that she was HIV positive. Distraught, she did her best to cope with the heavy burden on her own until her health took a huge turn for the worse during Ariana's junior year of high school.

She watched her mom go from being a proud, strong, independent black woman who took adversity head on, to a withered, beaten down woman barely holding onto life.

Had Ariana not stumbled across her mother's journal after witnessing her break down in tears at the kitchen table unable to complete what appeared to be a letter, she would have never known the severity of her condition.

As the painful reality of her mom being in the last stages of full-blown AIDS and not having much longer to live hit her, a mixture of deep sorrow and even deeper anger washed over her. Feeling betrayed by her mother for not sharing the information, she took her anger out in her performance at school.

At the time, Brittany and Sasha were her closest friends. After a few weeks of stewing over the news, she confided in them.

Unbeknown to her, Sasha pretended to be her friend because she was considered popular in school. A lot of guys wanted to get with her while a lot of girls wanted to be her. Seeing Ariana in such a vulnerable state, Sasha filled Quanetta in, who began to spread the gossip with her own spiteful twist. When Ariana found out Quanetta was behind the rumors, she brought a blade to school with intentions of taking a chunk out of her high cheekbones. Once again she made the mistake of confiding in her friends only to have Sasha tell the principal, who expelled her.

During her stay at Greenwood Alternative School, Ariana and Tavares grew close. According to her mom's standards, with his extracurricular street activities, he was bad news for her daughter.

Ariana knew there was much more to him if only he'd do something positive with his brilliant potential.
Outside of a distant aunt in South Carolina, Ariana didn't have family to turn to when her mom passed away two weeks before graduation. Tee ended up moving her into an apartment with him, took care of the formal

arrangements, and stayed by her side until she was ready to cope with the tragedy and move forward.

After Tee was incarcerated on his 18th birthday and sentenced, she felt as if her world was falling apart. Even with his crew making sure she didn't want for anything, nothing materialistic could replace the way Tee made her feel when they were together.

Making her way through downtown, she made a right onto Commerce St., and then turned left into the parking garage.

After navigating the winding ramp to the top, she instantly spotted Tavares in his usual spot. Parking next to him she took a deep breath before exiting the vehicle and walking over to him.

As she approached, Tee dismounted the ledge and met her with outstretched arms.

"Tee, I can't keep going through this," she sighed as her head settled on his chest.

"I know baby, I know."

"Do you really?" she said jerking away from him.

"If you really did you would quit acting like a statistic and do whatever it takes to be a father to our unborn son."

"Ariana, I couldn't agree with you more," he said taking a step closer. "As much as I want to provide for my family, I realize that I can't do nothing for y'all behind bars."

"So you're willing to leave all this nonsense behind?" she asked skeptically.

"Consider it dropped off in the same bin with the rest of that County clothing line."

"Tee, I'm serious. I love you and all, but I won't wait for you if I have to raise our son by myself."

"Well then I'll let y'all be the reason I never go back," he replied as he embraced her tightly before escorting her back to the car.

Pulling into the driveway, they exited the vehicle and made their way along the sidewalk and onto the porch.

Unlocking the door, Tee opened it wide for Ariana to enter, and then followed only to be stopped short at the landing.

"Wait right here," she said before running up the stairs and disappearing down the hall.

Perplexed, Tavares did as instructed. Moments later slow jams filled the eerie silence of the dark house followed by the sweet fragrance of vanilla candles put a smile on his face.

Growing restless he called out, "Baby you need any help up there?"

"I got this covered. For now just strip down and come up here so I can get that institutional stench off you," she demanded.

"Yes ma'am," he said as he eagerly complied. Entering the ocean theme bathroom illuminated solely by the animated moving picture mounted on the wall, Tee eased himself into the steamy water.

After soaking for a few minutes, Ariana sauntered in wearing fishnet stockings that led up to a black leather mini skirt with a cropped button up police shirt. As she approached, the clicking from her stilettos could be faintly heard over the soft music playing in the background.

"Mmm, come on over here and sentence me to life without parole," he said holding his wrists out. "I've been a bad boy."

"Be careful what you wish for," she replied as she playfully popped his hand. "Now prisoner, you have approximately 7 minutes to finish washing off and report to the bedroom. Dinner will be served promptly so bring your appetite."

"Anything else warden?" he said just before she turned to leave.

"As a matter fact there is. For the next 24 hours you're on lock down and for the remainder of the week, you'll be under my strict supervision."

"And if I misbehave?"

"After I finish with you, you'll be petitioning the governor to lock you up and melt the key. Now you're down to 5 minutes. I suggest you hurry Mr. Williamson," she said over her shoulder as she sashayed away.

{{{{{{{{{{{{{{{{{}}}}}}}}}}}}}}}}}}

Metropolis, Illinois

After what looked to be another uneventful evening of gambling, Donovan decided to cut his losses and retire.

Leaving the casino he was stopped short in the lobby.

"We need to talk!" Celeste demanded with her arms folded across her chest.

"Look, I had nothing to do with your friend's emotional breakdown," Donovan replied with his hands raised in a position of surrender.

"I am fully aware of that fact, which had it not been confirmed by her would have left you in a world of hurt."

Dismissing her threat, he attempted to brush past her unyielding frame only to be stopped short again.

"What part of 'we need to talk' don't you comprehend?" she snapped, causing a commotion in the lobby which made them become the center of attention.

Exhaling slowly Donovan responded, "Fine, say what you got to say then get the hell out my face. I got better things to do than become the main event for a bunch of spectators."

Noticing the scene she was making, Celeste took it down a few octaves. "Why are you avoiding her calls?"

"Are you serious? If you got the inside scoop like you claim then that should be painfully obvious."

"No, what's so obvious is that she has been stuck on your womanizing behind for way too long."

"Well she sure has a messed up way of showing it, and besides, that's her problem not mine. I kept it real with her from the jump; she's the one who flipped."

"I know and I'm not trying to make excuses for her actions, but with all she has been through, the least you can do is hear her out," she pleaded.

Seeing the determined look on her face he conceded, "If it means being able to lose my hard earned money in peace," he sighed.

"I had a feeling we would eventually see eye to eye. Now on behalf of the Harrah Casino, I would like to thank you for joining us this evening and we look forward to you visiting us again."

As Donovan merged onto I-24 leaving the Harrah Casino behind, he couldn't shake Naomi from his mind. After a few hours of debating whether or not to call, he gave in.

"Hello!" Naomi said out of breath from racing to the phone to pick it up on the 2nd ring. Then, trying not to sound desperate, she recovered, "Oh, it's you."

"Girl, stop playing like you ain't already know it was me."

"Whateva. I see you finally remembered my number. What you want anyway?" she asked with as much attitude as she could muster.

Seeing right through the facade he responded, "How about we leave the games to the kids and get our grown and sexy on." Catching her off guard he continued, "As you've probably already heard, I ran into your girl at the casino who so kindly informed me that you had something you needed to get off your chest."

After a brief pause she said, "Donovan, I don't know that I'd call it love, but I do know that I have felt strongly about you since we were back in high school."

"Why didn't you ever say anything?"

"For what? So I could wind up another notch on your belt? Please. Plus with all the tricks you had on your jock would you really have noticed me?"

"Hard to say, that depends on how real you would have come across."

"With the caliber of hoe's you were messing with, I highly doubt you know what real is."

"There you go assuming again. Put yourself in a man's shoes. If you had a bunch of females wanting to bop just because of your rep would you really deny them the honor?"

"Whateva. Y'all just nasty."

"If you say so, but one thing that I appreciated about you was that when you finally got up the nerve to approach me, you came off genuinely having an interest in getting to know the man behind the name."

"All that hype never really impressed me. If anything it just made me more insecure."

"So what about me did impress you?"

"Well I always thought you were kinda cute and smelled good, but what caught my attention was your sense of humor and fun loving nature."

"Awe, I think I'm starting to blush. Tell me more," he joked.

"See that's why you can't tell y'all big headed niggaz nothing."

"One thing I did notice about you in school was that you kept to yourself for the most part. Why was that Naomi?"

"I couldn't stand people always asking me what I was instead of who I was, as if I pulled up to school in a UFO. I used to sit in class, all nervous and afraid to answer questions with the right answer or pass with an A because of all the Korean jokes. I ain't even mixed with Korean!" she exclaimed.

"Yeah, I remember walking past your home room class and stopping to watch you go off on some chick for getting it twisted."

"It wasn't so much just them, step-dad added fuel to my rage and insecurity by constantly making it known that I wasn't his daughter. I was just the child his baby momma already had when he met her. He always treated me and my sister different growing up. Then as I got older he began to make remarks about my body that led to touching here and there until he finally couldn't hold that ugly beast ragging within. I was constantly in tears in my room with the music up or in the bathroom with water running, wanting high school to be over," she said emotionally.

"Dang shawty, I knew you had a few rough moments, but nothing to that extent. I don't know if I could have held my composure and went about my everyday routine like nothing was bothering me."

"It wasn't easy, but Celeste helped make things bearable by always having my back."

"How did y'all meet?"

"Well remember how I told you about the way kids in school used to ask me what I was? Well some of the more hateful girls used to pick on me regularly. Celeste happened to witness two girls trying to bait me into a fight so they could jump on me. Even though it wasn't her beef, she later told me that she had been in my shoes before and couldn't sit there and let me be victimized. Now at first glance, one would assume that Celeste was a slow big girl who at best could only grapple. But as many students found out, you should never judge a book by its cover," Naomi explained.

Celeste rose to her feet and shouted "Why don't y'all leave her alone!"

The girls took their attention off Naomi, who they had backed into a corner, with the bolder girl flipping Celeste the bird with her neck snaking back and forth as she said, "And what are you and those fat rolls gonna do about it?"

The other students turned and watched Celeste go from peacemaker to battle mode. Sensing they had bitten off more than they could chew the other girl attempted to reason with Celeste, "We ain't messing with you, so why you got to be all up in our bidness?" in a less than confident tone.

Stepping closer with both hands on her hips Celeste responded, "I'm making it my bidness." Not wanting any part of Celeste the timid girl backed away then bounced from the classroom leaving her bolder friend to fend for herself.

Nervous, but not wanting to punk out in front of the class, she stood her ground as Celeste called her out. "You always picking on girls prettier than your skank behind that you know won't fight back. Talk that ish now trick!" she said while mushing her in the forehead causing the entire class to burst out in laughter as they egged her on.

Surprisingly, the girl began to smile as the class went deftly silent with them sitting properly in their chairs. Hesitantly, she looked over her shoulder to see Assistant Principal Bedell standing over her.

"Ms. Evans, I need you to come with me."

Celeste ended up with Saturday school for 3 straight weeks, during which time we got close.

"Enough about me, tell me a little bit about you," Naomi said changing the subject.

"What would you like to know?"

"What was it like growing up with everyone admiring you and how did you get into the game?"

"Well for starters, I never knew my dad, and my mom passed away when I was twelve in a car accident. My mom was disowned for having me out of wedlock. I never knew the rest of my family and ended up in a group home."

"Oh baby, I'm sorry... I didn't know," Naomi said full of concern.

"It's okay, believe me you had it rougher than I did. I eventually ran away from the group home and hooked up with Tee who made sure I didn't go without. In the beginning he would sneak me leftovers and would talk his parents into letting me spend the night on weekends. During the week he would leave the window unlocked downstairs so that I could wash up and change clothes for the next day."

"That was nice of him."

"Tee was always real loyal. Even when his mom caught me red handed sneaking in, he took up for me when she was about ready to call the cops and have me picked up by Child Protective Services. I lived with him for the last two years of high school. He had it made with his father being retired military, working real estate and his mother as a teacher. There was no need for him to stress over getting money. But then again he was never the type to accept handouts so we got our grind on by boosting electronics from stores and selling them in school. As we got older, we began to dive deeper into the game chasing paper from hustle to hustle," he said, giving her the abbreviated version then changed the subject.

The conversation seemed to carry on for hours. As Donovan passed through Cadiz, his phone began beeping.

"As much as I've enjoyed this convo, I got low cell beeping in, so I'm gonna have to cut this short."

"Very cute," she replied sarcastically. "How far out are you?"

"About 45 minutes."

"Call me when you get settled in and low cell taken care of."

"I got you."

"You better. I'll be waiting up," she said just as the line went dead.

Crossing into city limits, Donovan decided to swing by the spot before heading home. As he turned onto the street and pulled into the driveway, a luminous feeling sent a tingle down his spine.

Shrugging it off, he drove around back and knocked on the door only to have it give way. Noting the fractured door frame, he withdrew the concealed .38 from his waist band and entered the ransacked house.

As he made his way through the grand kitchen and dining room, he almost stumbled over an unconscious body.

At a closer glance he recognized the bruised and badly beaten mass as belonging to Vince, Tony's cousin.

Quickly assessing that the intruders were long

gone he set out to survey the rest of the house. Upon entering the once lavish living room, he discovered Tony's body sprawled across the blood soaked pool table with his chrome .9 still clutched in his palm.

Infuriated, Donovan stormed over to Vince with a pitcher of water and doused him with it.

"Arrrgh!" he groaned trying to jolt upright.

"Come on, we got to get you out of here," he said helping Vince to his feet.

"What about Tony? We can't just leave him."

"That nigga was fam to all of us, but there's nothing we can do for him now," pausing to let his words sink in. "Now let's ride out so we can figure out who was behind this ambush," he said, assisting Vince into the car and driving off.

Chapter 6

As the first morning rays of sunshine began to seep through the blinds, Ariana slowly began to stir with remnants of last night's escapades running vividly through her mind.

Turning over on the satin sheets, she awoke with a start as she discovered Tavares was already gone. With all traces of ecstasy extinguished she angrily snatched her phone off the nightstand and dialed Tavares.

To her surprise his phone began ringing from the top of the dresser. As her curiosity took over, the fresh aroma of hot breakfast wafted upstairs and guided her to the kitchen where she found him making omelets.

"Ain't nothing like a man putting work in the kitchen," she said as she playfully smacked his buttock.

"Go on now and get back upstairs so I can treat you to some breakfast in bed."

"What, is it Mother's Day already or did someone catch a fever?" she said placing her wrist on his forehead.

"You got jokes, but if you plan on eating I'm gonna need you up out of my workspace so I can fine tune my cuisine skills."

"Baby, you mean culinary skills, cuisine is just a fancy word for food," she corrected.

"Now you're down to roughly 60 seconds and counting before I wrap up my culinary exhibit and start on the cuisine by myself."

"Alright already, just try not to burn down the kitchen."

Moments later Tee strolled into the bedroom imitating a butler as he proclaimed, "Breakfast is served Madam," with a slight bow. Then set up a TV table near the bed where he placed her omelet and OJ.

Just as he was propping up pillows behind Ariana to make her comfortable his phone began to ring.

"Now Mr. Belvedere, I know you aren't thinking about answering that while you are on duty," she joked with a slightly serious edge.

Remaining in character he replied, "Why of course not Madam."

Before she could reply the phone rang again. Frustrated she exclaimed, "Why the hell is someone blowing up your phone at 7 o'clock in the morning!"

"Don't get me lying," Tee said as he went to view the caller ID. Seeing it was Donovan he immediately knew something was up, which was confirmed by Donovan calling a 3rd time.

"Just answer the phone already," Ariana stated, clearly frustrated.

"What's good fam?"

"Tee, I know ya just getting settled in and all, but we need to talk."

"What can be that pressing at this hour?"

"It's pressing enough for us to have to meet up at the back up spot, ya dig?"

"Dang, that serious huh?"

"Mane, if you only knew the half of it."

"Okay give me an hour."

"Bet."

As the line disconnected, Tee slowly turned to address Ariana while his mind frantically searched for the rationale to explain his departure.

"You know what? Don't even bother with excuses," she spat.

"Baby it ain't like I planne-----" he uttered before she cut him off.

"I figured I'd get at least 24 hours of your undivided attention, but I guess that was way too much to ask. I don't even know why I waste my breath sometimes. Go on ahead nigga and play soulja boy in the streets and see if they keep you warm."

Opting to take flight rather than stay and fight, Tee quickly dressed and departed.

{{{{{{{{{{{{{{{{{{{}}}}}}}}}}}}}}}}}}}

Pulling into the parking lot at Finishing Touches Custom Detail Shop, Tee attempted to shrug off the apprehensiveness about the upcoming meeting.

Throughout the drive his mind replayed the various scenarios that could prompt an urgent meeting at the storefront.

After letting the engine idle for a brief moment to clear his thoughts, Tee stepped out of his gray Altima and walked past Donovan's champagne colored Tahoe on 24's to the back entrance. Inserting the key, he released the dead bolt, and then unlocked the door. Upon entering, he turned down the long corridor passed the supply room to the back office, where the trio was waiting.

"It's about time you broke free from Ariana's grasp," Roe stated.

"Whatever. Let's get this show on the road. I got home to take care of." Tee replied flatly.

Taking order Donovan announced, "Alright let's get down to the business at hand."

As Donovan described in detail the previous night's events the rest of the crew listened with feelings of shock, frustration, grief, and anger washing over their faces. The stash house being robbed and Vincent being beaten unconscious were losses they could have accepted, but Tony murdered, that was totally unacceptable.

"Them niggaz fend to have hell to pay for touching one of ours," Roe interjected to break the somber silence which was met by nods of agreement all around the room.

"First we need to figure out who was behind that ambush," Donovan stated.

"How we suppose to figure that out when they wore ski masks?" Chris asked.

"I say we crack a few skulls until someone delivers their names on a platter," Roe spat with malice in his eyes.

71

"Naw that ain't gonna do anything but bring more animosity and hatred from the streets that may come back to haunt us in the long run," Tee reasoned.

"So what do you propose we do?" Roe questioned.

"What if we put out a bounty on their heads?" Donovan proposed.

"That's a better approach, but I think it may be counterproductive," Tee stated.

"How so? Donovan asked. You got niggaz out here dropping dimes for much less than what we'd offer as a reward."

"Look at it this way, if you just hit a lick and knew there was a bounty on your head, unless you were as dumb as rocks you would lay low with your loot and gradually put them on the market or you would skip town." Tee explained.

"Let me get this straight. You think we should just let this ride?" Fired up Roe continued, "No disrespect fam, but I think you done let all that time spent in the poky dull that once sharp street edge you had."

"Don't get it twisted, that time ain't do nothing but make my mind sharper. With hard learned lessons comes wisdom, but stubbornness and failure to correctly assess situations is an indication of foolishness that results in self destruction."

Before Roe could respond, Donovan interjected, "As philosophical as this moment is, we need to come up with a unified decision..." When no one spoke up he continued, "how about we give it a few weeks before we put a bounty out to give those responsible time to get sloppy?"

"I'm with that. Once those snakes get complacent and stick their heads above the foliage, a little birdie is liable to spot em and deliver them to us for a reward," Tee stated.

"Then finally we'll get to go search and destroy mode, then leave their mangled bodies on the edge of our garden as an example of what happens when you jump stupid." Roe stated, as he rubbed his hands together plotting those responsible demise.

"Now that we got that settled, somebody toss me a flame so I can spark this blunt," Chris exclaimed.

"Y'all boys enjoy," Tee said, rising to leave as Chris inhaled the mid-grade smoke.

"Aiight fam, be easy," Donovan said to his back as he left the office.

As Tee approached his driveway, he noticed Ariana's car missing. Relieved, he pulled in and entered the side entrance of his 2-story brick house.

After pouring himself a double shot of Hennessey from the wet bar, he settled into his massage recliner in the den. Just as he made himself comfortable with the air bags rolling and kneading in all the right places and began flipping through his huge collection of DVDs, Ariana seemed to materialize on the stair landing and invade his personal space.

"It's about time you dragged your tail in here," she snapped.

"Where's your car?" he asked, trying to divert her attitude, but only added more fuel to the flame.

"I decided to park it in the garage for once because I figured your trifling behind would have taken longer to come back had you known I was here."

"Baby, that ain't it at all. I was just—"

Cutting him short, "The only thing you were just about to do was get on my last nerve... Now why is it that every time the streets call you go running? Am I that horrible of a person to spend quality time with? Do I not take care of your needs? Is there another woman?" she questioned.

Before she could shoot off another round of questions, Tee interjected, "Look, let's skip this game of

74

21 questions and get straight to the real answers that you should already know by now... Baby you not only take care of my needs, but also my wants and desires. I cherish the time we spend together, and hate it when something interferes with it. No one can captivate my interests like you and keep me wanting to come home night after night. I love you Ariana," he said sincerely.

"I love you too, Tee. I just get so worried sometimes when you're out there. And I know it's selfish of me, but I can't help wanting to spend most of my time with you."

"That's real baby. How about a change in scenery?" he asked.

"I'd love that. What do you have in mind?" she probed.

"You just worry about packing up a quick travel kit because we're hitting the road in thirty minutes."

Excited, Ariana threw her arms around Tee, kissed him passionately and took off upstairs to pack.

Meanwhile, Tee made a few phone calls to make arraignments. Within twenty minutes Vince pulled into the driveway.

"What's good fam?" Tee said greeting Vince with a pound.

"I know y'all handling things, but I should have been at the meeting today," Vince said, still steaming about losing his cousin.

"I feel ya pain, and no offense fam, but we knew you would have taken it the hardest out of everyone and with Roe already being his loose cannon self, we needed clearer minds to prevail." he reasoned.

"Just make sure, I get some of that payback before it's all said and done."

"You got it. Now where's the package?" he asked.

Opening the glove compartment, Vince reached in and pulled out a paper bag full of cash and handed it to Tee. "The ten grand is all there."

"Good looking out," Tee said as he quickly fanned through the bills and tossed Vince two grand. "I'll get up with y'all in a few days. Hold it down."

"Aiight fam be easy." Vince replied before pulling out the driveway.

Glancing at his watch, he shook his head and sighed to himself, "Women." Walking into the house he yelled up the stairs, "Baby, we gotta get on the road before we miss our flight."

"Don't rush me. I'll be down in a sec... Wait a

minute. Where are your bags? You did say we were traveling somewhere right?" she asked.

"Yeah and I also said to only pack a travel kit, meaning a few items that you needed to go from point A to B."

"You actually expect me to go out of town with just a travel kit?" she questioned. "You know I gotta have several outfits to change into along with my other necessities."

"There you go worrying about the wrong things. Can you let me do me and play the Big Willie role? I got your wardrobe and all the necessities you would need taken care of. Now come on we got less than an hour and a half before they start boarding."

After touching down at Piedmont Triad International Airport in Greensboro, NC, they walked through the bustling terminals until they reached the Avis counter. Once Tavares showed the agent his driver's license and credit card, he signed for the Chrysler 300 and they were on their way.

Having already established they were both famished, Tee followed N. Triad Blvd. until he navigated through traffic to High Point Rd. and pulled into the lot of the Sheraton Hotel. As they exited the vehicle and approached the hotel, Ariana paused to admire the beauty of the towering building reaching up into a skyline filled with hues of lilac, burnt orange, and sapphire.

"If you think this is something, wait till you see the inside," Tee said, picking up on her awe. Living up to the hype, Ariana was amazed at the splendor of the Hotel's lobby from its high polished marble floors, exquisite paintings and décor, and brilliant florescent lighting that brought the lobby to life. While Tee spoke with the receptionist, she picked up a brochure and read over the various amenities such as room service, indoor/outdoor pools, whirlpool, and spa in addition to a Concierge Club Lounge with the Four Seasons Shopping Mall within walking distance.

Engrossed into the brochure, she didn't even notice Tee sneak up behind her and place his arms around her waist with his lips nudging her ear he whispered, "So what do you have a taste for beautiful?"

"Depends, are you on the menu?" she playfully responded until her stomach started growling. "I guess I could go for some of this fresh sea food they're advertising at Joseph's Restaurant."

"Sounds like a winner," he replied kissing the back of her neck before leading her with their hands interlocked to the restaurant.

The hostess quickly seated them at a table near a window overlooking the pool and shortly afterwards the waitress came by to get their drink orders. Within minutes she returned with Ariana's virgin Strawberry Daiquiri and a bottle of Trefethen's Estate Dry Riesling white wine for Tee.

"Are you ready to order?" the waitress asked.

"I'm having a hard time deciding between the shrimp scampi and grilled salmon." Ariana stated.

"They are both really good, but my personal favorite is the grilled salmon," the waitress suggested.

"Okay then... I guess I'll give that a shot with a Caesar salad... Tee, have you decided yet?"

"Yeah, I think I'll go with the rib eye steak well done with a fully loaded bake potato."

"Alright then, if I could get those menus out of your way, I'll be right back with your salad," she said as she collected the menus then headed into the kitchen.

"Thank you, baby," Ariana said, placing her hand over Tee's hand. "I know I've been riding you hard lately about spending time with me. With the baby and all this extra drama that seems to be popping off my hormones seem to kick into overdrive at times causing me to overact."

"You're welcome beautiful and I forgive you."

79

"Who said I was apologizing," she said playfully pinching his wrist. "I'm carrying your seed; you best believe I'm entitled to my quality time."

"Dang, knowing I'm trapped for the next eighteen years ain't enough; you gotta be involved in every minute of that time. I think I'm trading you in for the baby momma 3000 model," he joked.

"Oh I got your baby momma 3000 alright. Keep playing and get stabbed," she replied reaching for the steak knife.

"Now you know I could never trade you in for a new make and model. After all the time and energy I've put into this relationship, I wouldn't take nothing short of Oprah for you."

"Nigga you must really be trying to get cut up. And to think later tonight I was gonna treat you like a king and let you have it your way," she said releasing his hand.

Before he could reply the waitress returned with her salad. "Your food will be finished in another moment. Is there anything else I can get you?"

"No we're fine," Tee said. After she walked away, he noticed Ariana staring at him intently, "Penny for your thoughts?"

"These will cost you much more than that."

"Name your price," he replied

"Honesty.....the whole truth and nothing but the truth."

"What, you think I got something to hide?"

"I just need straight answers," she said with her eyes locked onto his. "Why didn't you tell me that the ABM Cleaning Service laid you off?"

"I didn't want to stress you out about it. Not that I was getting paid for real in the first place, but that was legit money coming in that wouldn't eat at your conscience," he answered.

"I could have tried to help."

"I'm not good at asking for help, especially not from my woman."

"That male ego will have us sleeping on the streets."

"Do you have any idea how I feel? I try and I try and... when all the applications have been rejected without them even attempting to look past my record... it's like I'm a big failure who will never be anything more than the next weeks hustle."

"Having hard times doesn't make a man a failure," she reasoned.

"Either way you deserve better. I never wanted for you to inherit any of my problems and I fear the day that my drama becomes your drama..." Tee paused as the waitress brought out their main entrees and waited for her to leave before he continued, "Plus I know how you really feel about spending the money I make in the streets."

"Do you hear me complaining about it right now? Although math isn't my favorite subject I can put two and two together. With you working that janitorial gig only 3 hours a day, but coming home after a full 6 to 8 hour shift, I kind of figured you fell back into that lifestyle a while back."

"How did you find out about my hours?" Tee asked.

"Remember the first time we ran into your supervisor Duane at Wal-Mart and you introduced us? Well, a few months later I ran into him again in the checkout line and he made a comment about how he could count on you and the crew you got hired to have the PX clean by 9:30 so that y'all could clown around for the last 30 minutes before y'all had to clock out."

"So is that why you always assumed I was out creeping on you?"

"What do you think? You would come home night after night as if all you had been doing is work."

"Why didn't you ever confront me on what you heard?"

"I guess I was afraid of what I would find out."

"Baby, I apologize for deceiving you, but my motives were pure. I left for work early to find better job opportunities by day and stayed out late to ensure we kept a steady flow of income."

"How is the job search going?" she asked, relieved that Tee confirmed his faithfulness.

"It's going. I have another interview on Monday. I'm more than qualified for these positions I'm applying for, but they just won't see past my record, so from here on out I'm going by the 'even if they ask I won't tell' policy until I find someone willing to take a chance on me."

In that moment she saw what she loved about him. She didn't care if he owned a Fortune 500 company or worked the register at McDonald's. Wasn't about the money or the sex even though the sex was orgasmic. What she loved about him was plain and simple. He tried hard. He was a good guy. All good people had some bad in them, just like all bad people had some good in them. She'd seen the bad in him and she'd confessed the bad in her. "Tee, I just want you to know that I believe in you and am down to ride for you," she said sincerely.

"That means a lot to me. Now can we throw down on this scrumptious looking food before it gets cold?" he said, changing the subject.

"Oops, I almost forgot about your skinny tail having high metabolism. We better hurry up and get some food in you before they start taking snapshots for another feed the children commercial."

"You think you got jokes, but I done told ya about being politically correct. I ain't skinny, I'm lil boned."

"Whatever. Just feed your face so we can put some meat on them bones."

After stuffing themselves, they decided to walk it off by visiting the Four Seasons Shopping Mall. With Clarksville not having anything as extravagant as the three-story mall with over 150 stores, Ariana was in heaven. As she scurried between floors and department stores, Tee discreetly folded up a wad of bills and said, "Baby, go ahead without me. I gotta run to the restroom," as he wrapped his hands around her waist and slid the bills into her back pocket."

Already knowing Tee didn't have much stamina for shopping she replied, "Don't be too long, I wanna pick out something nice and get your opinion on it. You probably have a running itinerary of things for us to do. I need to make sure I'm dressed for the occasion."

"You know I got you..." he said, planting a kiss on her temple. "Now run along and I'll catch up," he continued as he gently smacked her backside.

Two hours and twelve shopping bags later, Ariana finally said she was ready to go back to the hotel. Had it not been for the mall closing within twenty minutes she probably would have shopped until Tee dropped.

Once they returned to the Sheraton and got settled into their suite, Ariana emerged from the bathroom wearing lingerie she had picked up earlier and sauntered to the king size bed where Tee awaited...

Chapter 7

With her mind occupied on Donovan in addition to her passing the supervisor test and first interview at work, Naomi realized she forgot to thank her friend for getting Donovan to give her another chance. After dialing the number Celeste picked up on the 2nd ring.

"It's about time you got back to me. I was just about ready to think the two of y'all hooked back up and eloped to Vegas or something," Celeste joked.

"Never that, at least not without bringing my maid of honor."

"Enough already. Tell me how things went."

After filling her in with the details of their conversation, they began to reminisce about Tavares' birthday party.

As the DJ played Rock Star a few girls rushed towards Donovan so that the whole room could see them dancing with one of the hottest guys at the party, on one of the hottest tracks at the moment, so everyone could envy them.

Thinking she didn't have a chance at dancing with him, Celeste and Naomi went to sit at the bar.

"Look at all those desperate hoes," Celeste said

shaking her head. "They have no class."

Nodding in agreement, Naomi added, "I'm not gonna play myself for nobody," as Quanetta walked up to Donovan and began pulling at him to no avail. He paid her no mind as he sidestepped her while his eyes scanned the room. Finding what he was looking for he moved through the crowd in their direction.

"OMG!" Celeste exclaimed, "I think he's coming over here."

"Yeah right, he probably just wants a drink," Naomi said, downplaying her excitement.

When he reached them he stood directly in front of Naomi and said, "You were looking real fly on the floor earlier. You wanna dance?" Shocked, Naomi couldn't believe what she was hearing, but before she could respond Tony materialized from nowhere and pulled Donovan to the side. Seeing the urgency in which Donovan along with the rest of his entourage left the party she knew something had to be going down.

"Dang gurl you were so close," Celeste said patting her girl on the back.

{{{{{{{{{{{{{{{{{{{{{{{{{{0}}}}}}}}}}}}}}}}}}}

Waking up late that afternoon, Ariana and Tee made their way back to Joseph's for brunch before heading out for a day of fun at Wet 'N Wild Emerald Pointe Water Park.

"So where do you wanna start?" Tee asked after they paid the admission and entered the park.

"It's been too long since I've done anything like this. I wish I could ride the thrill rides," she said rubbing her belly.

"Mane, I didn't even think about that," Tee said disappointingly. "Guess we are gonna have to hang out in the kiddy pool."

"How about I watch you take on a few fast paced rides then we relax together on some of the slower ones," Ariana said, knowing Tee's thrill seeking side was amped up.

"Bet," Tee said as he jumped in line at the Blue Streak. Blowing her a kiss he descended down the enclosed water slide that sped straight down, twisted and turned, then went loop the loop. Followed by the Banzai Pipeline at speeds of 40 miles an hour, he fell down five stories on an inner tube that felt like being on a roller coaster and a waterfall combined into five seconds.

Feeling breathless afterwards, he waited in the long, but fast moving line for the White Water Run which featured the Twister, Dragon's Tail, and Easy Rider five story high water slides that twisted and turned him on an exhilarating plunge into the refreshing splash down pool below.

"Alright, I think I'm ready to slow it down a bit."

"Awe, come on dare devil. Old age ain't catching up to you is it?" she taunted.

"I see you got jokes. Well I bet this old mane still has enough energy to swim against Niagara Falls currents," Tee replied as his eye grazed over Ariana's frame hungrily.

"I can't take you nowhere without you trying to cut up," she said playfully.

"I'll come back to this one later. Let's chill out on those comfortable looking inner tubes on the Lazee River and ride the current."

As the gentle ride around the water park came to an end, the duo disembarked and hit up a few more rides before splashing about in the gigantic wave pool.

When the sun began to make its descent through the heavens, Tee guided Ariana away from the onslaught of crashing waves and dried her off. "That was fun. I can't wait to bring our baby here. Did you see the kiddy area?" she said, rubbing her belly.

"Yeah, I can just see him trying to climb up the

side of the volcano and go down the slide."

"You're really confident this is going to be a boy. How would you handle a daddy's girl being our new arrival?"

"Considering all I shoot out is Y chromosomes, that question is irrelevant. Now let's get out of these wet clothes and into something worthy of a night on the town. We got moves to make."

{{{{{{{{{{{{{{{}}}}}}}}}}}}}}}

Back in Clarksville, Roe and Chris rode from hood to hood in search of his missing ride.

"Nigga, I hope you plan on compensating me for all this riding around. You know gas ain't cheap. How did you get your ride stolen anyway?" Roe asked.

"Mane, I messed up and left the keys in the ignition while me and Quanetta were going at it inside the house."

"You've got to be one stupid mofo. Why the hell is you still worried about her anyway?"

"Because she's the one for me. I can't really explain it other than you've got to love the ones that love you back."

"If that ain't the corniest line I ever heard. That hoe doesn't even love you."

"Watch ya mouth mane, you don't know her like that," Chris said defensively.

"I may not, but anyone willing to drop off a bill to a buck fifty can know her anyway they want."

"Take that back!" Chris said, enraged.

"Or else what?" Roe challenged. "You is one blinded love sick puppy. I was at Tippers with Donovan when she tried to get at him. After he shot her down, she put her own self on blast about how she thought Donovan was man enough for her, but she was wrong and how most niggas got to come off bread just to lick her twat much less get the pussy she was throwing at him."

"And how long ago was this?" Chris questioned.

"About a week or so before you started bragging about how you finally got it."

"Whatever. I just know whoever stole my ride fend to have hell to pay," Chris said, changing the subject.

As they turned down Paradise Hill Rd., Roe spotted it at the corner store. "Looks like its pay day...

You ready to dish out hell?" he said, pointing toward the car.

"Let's get it," Chris said, while trying to psych himself up. "How do you want to go about it?"

"Real fast and violent." Seeing the perplexed look on Chris' unsure face, he continued, "Look, just jump out the car and aim ya strap at him as soon as he gets behind the wheel."

Finally, Squeak casually strolled out the store with a Grape Swisher Sweet cigarillo behind his ear and a plastic bag filled with items to cure the munchies. As he unlocked the door and slid behind the wheel, Roe made his move. Before Squeak knew it, Roe's blue Skylark was parked bumper to back door with him pinned in by two cars on each side.

"Run up on that fool!" Roe shouted as Chris clumsily exited the vehicle with his gun drawn.

"Put your hands where I can see em," Chris said as Squeak glared at him with contempt.

"Screw you!" Squeak replied as he blatantly made a move for his pistol tucked between his seat and middle compartment. Chris nervously attempted to squeeze off a round into his skull, but realized he had never bothered to take the safety off. Just as Squeak began to raise his pistol, Roe's .357 shattered the passenger's window and planted a round into Squeak's shoulder causing him to drop the pistol.

"Look at my freakin' window! I had it under control!" Chris exclaimed, while Squeak grimaced in pain.

"Like hell you did... now quit crying and knock that nigga out!" Roe ordered. Tentatively Chris complied... "Mane, if you don't hurry up, I swear I'll come over there and put both y'all to sleep in the trunk," Roe threatened.

As the pistol grip collided with his skull a third time, Squeak slumped over the steering wheel.

Forcefully, Roe swung open the door and drug him out of the car. "Pop the trunk and help me lift this clown." With the body tucked away, Roe hopped back into the Skylark while Chris scrambled to get in his green Ford Focus and catch up to Roe who was already pulling off.

Merging onto Highway 79 from 41A, Chris' breathing didn't become easier until they finally crossed the bridge into Dover County. Veering off onto a side road, Chris continued trailing Roe as his mind wondered what torture he had in store for him before he put Squeak out of his misery. Slowing to a halt at a natural made cul-de-sac surrounded by a canopy of trees, they opened the trunk to find their victim beginning to stir.

"Rise and shine... time to die south sucka," Roe taunted as they snatched him out and made him stumble through the woods until he tripped and fell to his knees.

"I ain't walking another step... y'all lames do what ya gotta do," Squeak spat.

"Handle ya bidness mane," Roe said glancing towards Chris.

"Me?" he questioned.

"Roe, I don't even know why you bringing this boy to a grown man's arena. He couldn't even take care of his girl without us gang banging that thick booty to make sure she got hers much less pull a trigga... Old scary lame boy," Squeak taunted.

"I'll show you a lame boy," Chris snarled as he pointed his piece at him clicking the safety off in the process and unloaded six rounds in him before Roe stepped in.

"Chill fam, that nigga dead and gone. Let's raise up out of here," he said motioning towards the cars.

With his mind on autopilot, Chris didn't come out of his daze until he was alone in his apartment complex parking lot. "What have I done?" he sighed to himself as the after effects of remorse and anguish washed over him.

{{{{{{{{{{{{{{{{{{{0}}}}}}}}}}}}}}}}}}}}

Meanwhile as Tavares cruised down I-40, Ariana took a well-needed nap. Without her chatting away about their future together, Tee's mind began to relive the past. Just five years ago, he was making runs through the Carolinas to Georgia and Tennessee learning the distribution trade from Blanc. With his drive and ambition, Tee was soon getting points off the package to deal directly with Q who ran things in Georgia and Trust who held down the Carolina's with his right hand man Mac the enforcer.

Gaining their trust over the course of a year, they showed mad love from putting him up in expensive hotels, lending him fly rides to stunt in, and V.I.P treatment wherever they went.

Passing through Half Moon on Gum Branch Rd., Ariana began to stir, "Are we there yet?" she asked breaking his trance.

"Almost... just another 5 minutes."

"Good, pull over somewhere. Your baby is elbowing the hell out of my bladder."

"Can't it wait till we get to the club?" Seeing the icy stare she gave, "Okay," he conceded, pulling into Amoco/McDonald's parking lot.

Once she returned, they drove the short distance down Western Blvd. to the Planet Rock nightclub, which had a line, wrapped halfway around the building.

"Please tell me we don't have to wait in that long line." she whined

"Chill baby, you know I got this..." he said as he finished up a text message. "Just follow me." He finished getting out of the car. As they walked past the line, some made sly comments while others stared on with envious eyes. Reaching the front entrance security put a quick halt to their forward progress to the enjoyment of the haters in line.

"Y'all got to wait, just like everyone else," he snorted pointing to the end of the line.

"Mane, do what you got to do to get a hold of Trust," Tee said eying down the guard.

Just as he was preparing to reiterate himself, Trust materialized, "I know you ain't harassing my special guests," he said embracing Tee. Before the bouncer could reply he continued, "Let's get up to V.I.P area so you can catch my new artist perform... Oh, and let me guess. You must be the lovely Ariana that I hear so much about," he added as he lightly shook her hand and nodded his approval to Tee.

Trust introduced them to Courtney, his new wifey, as they settled in upstairs. While waiting on their drink orders to arrive, Big O took the stage performing his smash single 'Matics' with the crowd fully engaged as they sang the hook along with him. Just as the song was coming to an end, the beat changed and two guys came out of the crowd with wireless mics and jumped on stage to perform 'We Came To Party' which hyped the crowd even more.

When the set ended, Lick em Low got on stage with the wireless mic and got the crowd to give them one more round of applause before turning the DJ loose.

"So what did you think?" Trust asked while Ariana and Courtney made small talk.

"Ya boys did their thing. You got em signed yet?"

"In the process. Trying to decide between two labels showing a lot of interest."

"When you get the chance you need to peep this out," Tee said reaching into the front cargo pocket of his Giraud jeans and pulling out a CD.

"Any good?"

"I wouldn't waste your time with it if it wasn't," Tee responded.

"Alright, after I get a feel for it, I'll see what I can do with it," Trust said, taking the CD and giving it to Courtney to put in her purse.

"Bet, so where's Mac?" Tee asked scanning the club.

"He's helping Q with a lil situation out in Augusta right now, but should be back next week."

"I see y'all boys still going hard."

"No choice but to go hard, especially with these young niggas out here acting like they don't know how to respect those that's been getting money."

"Sounds like someone else I once knew," Tee said cutting his eyes at Trust.

After the two of them caught up on old times, Tee took Ariana to the dance floor for a while before departing to the Fairfield Inn for the evening. With their plane scheduled to depart midafternoon, they allowed sleep to overtake them.

Chapter 8

The next evening, Quanetta and Sasha, chauffeured by their girl Free, pulled up in front of the Gentleman's Club. Already late they hurriedly grabbed their gear and pushed their way through the thick crowd. Finally arriving at the dressing room they were greeted by Diamond and Champagne putting on an exhibition as their tongues swirled and sensually traveled over each other's bodies.

Realizing they now had an audience, their passion intensified as coos and moans escaped their lips, until Quanetta interrupted their flow. "Y'all sluts are lousy spokes models for lesbians. If this were a commercial designed to get me to cross over, then y'all would have failed miserably."

"Whatever. With that soft prissy nigga that be on your arm, you might as well be dating a woman. Come on Diamond. Let's get this paper from these real niggas out here making money," Champagne taunted as they left the dressing room.

Quanetta shot her the evil eye then addressed Sasha. "Ya know that raggedy pussy trick just mad because I wouldn't let her lick my twat."

"Yeah, she been eye balling you for a while as if the more she stare and dance next to you the more inclined you'll be to take her up on her offer," Sasha replied as the duo put on their outfits.

Unbeknown to them Diamond had doubled back for the nightstick to complete her cop theme. Lurking on the opposite side of the lockers she heard them disrespect her soul mate and was on the brink of defending her with a few choice insults until Quanetta switched topics...

"I know one thing for sure, I can't wait till I can drop Chris' lame behind like last month's tampon."

"After hanging with you for one day I can see why you have two phones with one just being for his annoying tendencies."

"You don't even know the half of it. If it weren't for the money, I would have been cut him off."

"I thought you said he wasn't nothing but a budget wanna be baller that was only able to front like he was getting money because he grew up with HPC."

"Girl, I wasn't referring to those table scraps he throws me that barely pay my phone bill and rent. I make three times as much by relaying the info that motor mouth tells me about their crew to interested parties," Quanetta explained.

"Is that how them stick up boys got the jump on HPC last week?"

"They would have never known where the stash spot was had Chris never given me a grand tour of the place."

"You know Tony got killed behind it?"

"Forget them. I could care less about doing niggaz dirty. They'd do it to me if I let them or if it benefited them to try. Just like this strip game I ain't looking fa love, I'm looking fa money."

"I heard that so, what you wearing tonight for your solo?" Sasha asked as she pulled up her black fishnet stockings to match her black thong and stilettos.

"You'll see..." she replied as she slipped into a dark green thong. "Its money out there and them niggaz drunk and horny."

"Yeah, let's go ahead and take advantage of them feeling real generous," Sasha replied as they applied the finishing touches to make them irresistible.

As they stepped out of the dressing room and into the club they began to solicit their bodies to patrons. Sasha found one customer who was more than happy to come up off $20. In return she pushed his back against the wall and turned around; pressing her backside against his manhood then began to throw it at him. Like an octopus his hands were all over her groping any part of her body not pressed against him.

103

Meanwhile, Diamond, having overheard their conversation, slipped out of the dressing room and hurriedly found Champagne.

"Girl you ain't gonna believe what I heard that trifling trick admit to in the dressing room..." After filling Champagne in, a devious grin spread across her exotic face.

"Ya know HPC has a reward out for info on who stuck up their spot."

"Yeah, I heard about that. Do you know how to get up with any of them?" Diamond asked.

"I used to have Roe's number, but you know how them type of niggas be switching up," Champagne replied.

"We need to jump on this before someone else cashes in on our opportunity."

"Wait a sec; I can get at Tee's girl through Lashay. Come on lets go backstage. I need you to her make sure ain't nobody eavesdropping."

"I got you."

Hours quickly passed and it was soon Quanetta's time to go on stage in the spotlight for her grand performance. After returning from the dressing room

104

with her army camouflage hot pants, matching bra, and camouflage stilettos, she hit the stage where she dipped, turned, and then interlocked her legs around the pole, bending backward then sliding down the pole into a handstand. After reaching the ground and getting back to her feet, slowly she began to unfastened her outfit and seductively drop it to the ground as she wound her hips panning the crowd with a pointed finger.

Now she was nude, except for her camouflage garter, stilettos, and gloves. With her audience captivated she bent over, using the pole for support then began to make her cheeks bounce before she elegantly dropped to the floor in the split position giving the room a full view of her touching herself which sent them into frenzy. After several different poses the DJ hollered into the mic, "Dis ain't a free show! Tip the lady!"

As Quanetta panned the floor again with her index finger she noticed a hooded female walking toward the stage. Assuming it was just a dike feeling her swag she decided to play up the moment by beckoning her toward the stage to join her.

Once she reached the edge of the stage, Quanetta sensually gyrated her hips as she glided toward her.

As she neared the lone figure, she called out, "I hope you got a big tip for this special show I'm fend to put on for ya ma."

"I sure do ya scandalous trick!" she replied removing her hood. As recognition etched across her face, Ariana launched a zip lock bag full of quarters at her face drawing blood as the bag smashed into her nose.

Before Quanetta could recover Brittany came from out of the shocked crowd and began to pounce on her.

Seeing her girl getting jumped Sasha ran up on the melee only to have Lashay crack her over the head with a half empty Corona bottle.

For Quanetta and Sasha the beat down seemed to last a life time, but in actuality they didn't receive half of what the trio had in store as payback due to the club's bouncers rushing in and separating the two parties. When it was all said and done, hair extensions, tracks, and blood lay on the floor while Ariana, Lashay, and Brittany left the club hurling insults and threats.

The girls sat around a bedroom at Brittany's house reliving the fight.

"Those tricks finally got what they deserved!" Lashay exclaimed.

"Yeah, Sasha really had that beat down coming for years," Ariana said, remembering their last altercation at Tee's birthday party.

"What do you think Tee gonna say about you

106

fighting while you're carrying his seed?" Brittany asked.

"Ain't much he can say except him being disappointed with the way he still running around these streets doing dirt in the name of being a family man. Plus, because of that trifling hoe, our QT got cut short."

"I wouldn't be so hard on him. You know with his record it ain't easy to find a good job in this dead end town where the only decent work is either in a factory or working for Uncle Sam," Brittany replied.

"I don't see why you don't just set that nigga loose in the streets again to get money. Y'all used to live real lavish versus fretting over making ends meet," Lashay questioned.

"I ain't gonna lie, the money was good and all, but what matters most to me is knowing that at the end of the night he's coming home to me and not to a jail cell or the ground."

"I would never mess with no celebrity or drug dealers, because they have too many girls sweating and hawking them. You would always have to wonder if they out screwing around... naw... not me," Brittany said shaking her head adamantly.

"Gurl, you crazy! I would get with one of them hood rich boys in a second, cause niggaz gonna cheat regardless, so I would rather be with a rich cheating nigga, shopping and spending his money while he out boning some hoe, than being at home broke while he sowing his oats!" Lashay exclaimed.

"You a hoe," Brittany replied. Lashay started grinding her hips and rubbing her thumb and index finger together, "Yeah, but I be a paid hoe."

"Don't you ever get tired of messing with so many dudes?" Ariana asked.

"Look girl, sometimes it's too much to stay involved too long... people want so much from each other. Sometimes it's nice to be with somebody who don't want anything more than you're willing to give," Lashay explained.

"Enough about miss nasty over there. So tell us how your vacation went!" Brittany said eagerly.

"Yeah, I remember you saying you left in a hurry with no bags and now you have three unpacked suit cases, so I already know you went on a shopping spree. Did you pick me up anything?" Lashay asked.

"Shut up and let her tell the story already. I bet it was romantic," Brittany said.

As Ariana described their vacation in detail, Brittany and Lashay listened intently while wishing they had someone special to share a moment like that with.

Chapter 9

News of the altercation at the Gentleman's Club spread like wild fire through the streets. It seemed like everyone and their momma found out about it the next day with the exception of Tavares.

As Gio was working on trimming Tee's goatee at Keesee's Barber Shop on College St., Watts strolled in from making a food run.

"What's good Tee... I heard ya girl went WWF hardcore champion on some hood rats the other night," Watts said as he separated the orders and distributed them.

"Yeah, I was there mane. Ya girl was in rare form, but you would have been proud by the way she handled bidness," Carlos added.

"When and where was this?" Tee asked feeling out of the loop.

"Dang, I figured you were the mastermind behind it," Watts said.

"Naw, I think I missed the memo... Los would you be kind enough to clue me in?"

After colorfully describing the highlights of the girl fight that had the other barbershop patrons listening intently, Tee did his best to conceal his shock and disbelief.

"I guess she must've had it coming," Tee said downplaying the seriousness of the incident.

"You can say that again. I don't know how accurate this is, but they say Quanetta was somehow in on that robbery that got ya boy Tony laid out," Cedric chimed in.

With his mind now on the defensive and kicking into overdrive, Tee ran through a gauntlet of scenarios with all roads leading to Dee somehow being responsible. Initially, when Ariana had told him about her running into Dee at the movie theater, he had figured it was by coincidence and that he was just taking that opportunity to intimidate her. Upon further reflection Tee knew that he couldn't put anything past Dee's treacherous mind. Concluding with that variable in the mix, Tavares knew what had to be done to protect the ones he loved.

As Gio finished swabbing his hairline and face with alcohol and brushing him off, Tee remembered he had brought the numbers for his music marketing campaign.

"Hey fam, I almost forgot to update you on your number of plays for the week," Tee said reaching into his pocket and handing Gio, who performed under the name

Phantom, his stats. "As you can see 'Rock Star' and 'Chevy's & Lacs' are fan favorites."

"That's the bidness," Gio said proudly as he looked over his ever-increasing number of plays and comments from his custom built website. "I appreciate you taking the time to manage my site for me."

"I can't even take all the credit for it anymore. With all those referrals you sent my way, I had to hire a small team to manage the other artists' profiles."

"The power of networking. We just need to keep pushing until something happens."

"Speaking of networking, I just got back from a lil vacation in North Carolina where one of my home boys is a big time DJ. He rubs elbows with a lot of mainstream industry types and makes radio appearances here and there. I slid him a mix featuring your hottest tracks and told him to see what he could do with it."

"Good looking out mane, I'ma get up with you a little later on in the week to get that music video uploaded."

"That's what it is. Be easy fam," Tee said dapping him up before he turned to leave.

Once settled in his car he pulled out his phone. "What's good?" Donovan answered on the 3rd ring

"Is the Oak Grove cut still clean and free?" Tee asked.

"Yeah, what you got in mind?"

"Meet me over there in about twenty minutes and I'll brief you on the situation."

"Aiight," Donovan said before disconnecting the line...

{{{{{{{{{{{{{{{{{}}}}}}}}}}}}}}}}}

"You sure this is what you want?" Donovan questioned Tee after hearing him out.

"What choice do I have...? You already know Ariana ain't the type to back down from a threat and I couldn't live with myself if something happened to her because of my drama."

"How you figure she gonna skip town after y'all break it off?"

"Outside of me and a few friends ain't nothing here for her. Ya know her pops passed away back in high school and her mom joined him while I was locked up. She's threatened me before with moving back to South Carolina where the majority of her family lives," Tee explained.

112

"So you think this will push her over the edge to make that move? I think she's liable to make a move upside your head. You know pregnant women get unstable when their emotions get messed with."

"It is what it is. I love her enough to let her go than to see her and my seed harmed or destroyed."

"Aiight, I don't like it but you like a brother to me and I support you no matter what," Donovan said handing over the keys to Tee.

"Thanks. In the meanwhile, can you drum up a few soldiers to watch the crib until this drama plays out?"

"Say no more. We'll make sure the castle stays secure."

"So what's the deal with you and Naomi?" Tee inquired.

"Hard to really say at this point. We connected on so many different levels and I haven't even hit that yet."

"Huh... are you feeling okay?" Tee said playfully, feeling Donovan's head for a fever. "This can't be the same pimp I grew up with."

"It's kinda complicated, but I ain't even tripping over that with her. Tonight we are supposed to take it there."

"You must really be feeling her."

"Yeah, but it's way too early in the game to let her know I'm starting to catch feelings. Once they think they got you, they tend to switch up sometimes."

"Is that it or are you still afraid of commitment?" Tee asked.

"I wouldn't say all that. I just ain't ready for commitment yet. Now can you get off your soap box Doctor Phil. I got errands to run."

"Whatever, Mr. In-Denial. Just make sure I'm your best man when it's all said and done," he joked.

"Now I'm really out before you go Miss Cleo and start predicting kids," Donovan said heading for the door.

{{{{{{{{{{{{{{{}}}}}}}}}}}}}}}

Later that evening as Naomi traveled down I-24, thoughts of Donovan filled her mind. As impressed as she was with his patience on them consummating their relationship, she felt it was time for her to allow him to stimulate her body just as he had been doing her mind for months.

114

Nearing exit 11, she listened to the sounds of "Fairy Tale" and "One Night in Town" by Same Differences resonating through her speakers as she envisioned what it would be like to give into her desires.

After knocking on the door, she heard Donovan call out, "Come on in." Upon opening it she was greeted by shimmering candles placed throughout the house with soft romantic music playing in the background and began to smile to herself as she took notice of the white rose petals leading through the living room and up the winding stair case. Following the trail to where they stopped at the bathroom door, she slowly twisted the knob and eased the door open to find Donovan sitting in a Jacuzzi filled with rose petals.

"Baby, you really didn't have to go all out like this," she said, trying to keep from blushing.

"Shhhh... I wanted to make tonight special... There's a bottle of champagne in the ice bucket."

Why don't you pour yourself a drink and join me?" Kicking off her shoes, she did a slow strip tease to prolong the moment, which Donovan let her know he thoroughly enjoyed. Then she walked over to the sink and grabbed the bottle of champagne and a glass. From there, she eased her foot into the tub, trying to adjust to the heat of the foaming water.

"Oooh, Donovan this feels so good."

"If you think this feels good, you ain't seen nothing yet." Donovan licked his lips suggestively.

"Is that right? What you got for me?" she asked eagerly.

"Come on in here and find out." He lifted his eyebrows in that sexy way she loved.

First, pouring herself a glass, she then eased into the Jacuzzi completely. "Okay, I'm here. The next move is yours," she teased.

"I'm about to take deep sea diving to another level." He smiled then dove under the water. The next thing she knew, his head was between her legs and she was holding onto the sides of the Jacuzzi moaning loudly.

Slowly emerging from the water he gazed at her with lust filled eyes as she returned his with hers filled with pent up desire. Scooping her up in his toned arms he carried her into his bed where they kissed like they couldn't get enough of each other.

"Oh, Donovan," she whispered repeatedly, clinging to his back as she climaxed.

"Yeah, baby, that's it." He was kissing her neck and was about to make her climax again.

"I...I love you Donovan. I love you more than anything in this world," she cried out as she became overcome by yet another orgasmic wave. Even in her moment of ecstasy she noticed that he did not reciprocate her confession of love.

Although she had originally wanted him to be the first one to say it, the champagne and mesmerizing sex had loosened up her tongue. The air turned still. She could tell by his rigid posture that he was caught off guard by her confession, but she couldn't hold it any longer and desperately wanted to hear him tell her the same.

"I love you Donovan," she repeated. For the past month she had been hoping to entice him into saying it first, but at this point she would have settled for a "me too."

"Naomi, I'm not gonna lie to you..." She could tell by the look in his eyes that she didn't want to hear whatever he was about to say, so she placed her index finger to his lips.

"Shhhh. I know we have only been dating a couple of months. You don't have to say it back," she lied. "I just wanted you to know how I feel." She rested her head on his shoulder.

"Naomi," he whispered a few seconds later.

"Yes," she whispered back, trying to contain her excitement. She had been feeling he was about to say those magical words.

"I really care about you and like you a lot, but can't honestly say that I love you. I'm just not ready to commit myself to saying those words you're looking to hear right now. Who's to say though that in the near future these strong feelings I have for you don't fester into something more," he said bringing hope as he leaned over and kissed her.

Chapter 10

As the days began to turn into weeks, Ariana noticed she was seeing less and less of Tee.

Granted, she figured he had a lot of catching up to do from their weekend getaway. However, this was ridiculous. Not only was he hardly home and rarely called to check in, but even when he was home, he was very distant. Getting any convo was like pulling teeth, much less some genuine attention.

Despite several attempts on her to spice things up in the bedroom, Tee only expressed minimal interests in showing any affection.

With insecurity and anxiety mounting over the past four nights of no contact at all, Ariana set out to confront Tee. Having visited a few of his known chill spots and turning up empty handed, she rode aimlessly from Franklin St. to Main St. until she happened upon 9th St. As she was preparing to halt for the red light at the College St. intersection, she spotted his car in the back parking lot.

Turning sharply into the front lot, Ariana stormed into the College St. Barbershop in search of Tee.

"Is everything okay Miss?" Reese asked.

"It will be once I find Tee. I know he's here.

Where is he?" she said trying to remain calm.

"I think you may have just missed him," Kenny responded in an attempt to cover up.

Shooting him a dark glare that let him know she was no fool, she walked out the back entrance and walked around the side of the building to find Tee and Phantom conversing.

"Tavares!" Ariana yelled. "Where have you been? I didn't know if you were dead or alive!"

As if it was no big deal, he shrugged, "I was taking care of some business."

Ariana frowned, "You so busy that you can't pick up a phone and check up on me? I'm due in four months; you could at least show some concern."

Although he wanted to scoop her in his arms and tell her how much she had been on his mind lately and how he wanted to give her the quiet life she wanted, he knew what had to be done. "Look," Tavares said, "I'm grown and don't need you clocking me."

Bewildered, Ariana looked at him, "Tee, what's gotten into you? Why are you talking to me like that?"

"Because I can," he barked. "Now roll out and leave me be before I really turn ghost on you."

"Tee, I'm just seeing if you are okay, because I haven't heard from you in over a week!"

"Now you see me," Tee snapped. "Now you can take your emotional act home!"

"When are you coming home?" she asked, surprised.

"When I get ready. As a matter of fact, what you need to do is find you someplace else to live cause I ain't feeling this anymore."

Tears filled her eyes, "Are you serious?"

He looked her straight in the eyes, "As serious as your dad infecting your mom with AIDS!"

"Screw you!" she said slapping his face so hard that his neck recoiled. "I gave you my all and this is how you repay me. You don't have to worry dodging home anymore. By the time you finally decide to stop by every trace of me being there will be gone." Staring at him in disbelief, then slowly backing away, she clutched her body as if to hold it together. She fought to hold back the tears, but lost that battle when she got around the corner.

{{{{{{{{{{{{{{{{{}}}}}}}}}}}}}}}}}

Meanwhile, right around the corner, Roe and Chris were engaged in a heated argument about the previous night's drama.

Chris having pumped his veins full of that liquid courage from Callee's and still amped up from getting his ride back had begun running off at the mouth as if King Kong didn't have anything on him.

"I wish a nigga would try to get out of line! I ain't the one!" he shouted to everyone within earshot at the Dodge Store.

"Chill your drunken self out mane," Roe said, trying to pull at his arm.

"Bump that ish!" he exclaimed, breaking free from Roe's grip. "I'll make these weak boys either get down or lay down." He continued to rant as he jammed his index finger into the temple of a short, slim guy who was on his way back to the car.

"Ease the hell back," the guy calmly stated to Chris as he pushed his hand away.

"And what if I don't?" Chris said, jumping back in his face. Had Chris not been so drunk, he might have realized the guy he was agitating was a hard body, no nonsense, enforcer by the name of Junior.

Without warning, Junior whipped out a chrome Beretta and jammed the muzzle into Chris's stomach.

"Didn't I tell you to piss off," he growled.

Shaking his head in disgust, Roe pulled out a glock and trained it on him, "Junior, you already know I can't let it go down like that."

"Stay out of this Roe. It's time for this fool's check to bounce," he replied while Chris stood there wide eyed with the barrel pressed against his belly button.

"Not on my watch," he replied with his gun still holding Junior in his sights.

Although there was mutual respect, each man knew that sooner or later their paths would cross. "You know you out gunned right now," Junior said as four gunman materialized through the crowd of onlookers.

"I peeped the math before you even brought up the equation. I suggest you take a second look and reassess the situation," Roe challenged as two of his associates disarmed Junior's back up.

The odds, now even, with Junior and his two remaining gunmen ready to set it off with Roe and his two associates, the crowd began to quickly disperse. Almost on cue, two police cruisers pulled into the parking lot.

"Til next time chump," Junior said through gritted teeth as he eased his Beretta into his waistband before

123

turning to join his comrades who had already fled to the car and had it running. He glanced back at Roe and said, "You really need to watch the company you keep."

Knowing his words were ringing true, he nodded out of respect then yelled, "Bring yo petrified self on before I leave you in your own car," while Junior joined his crew and vacated the premises.

"I know what I did last night was stupid," Chris admitted.

"Stupid ain't even the word for it. Had my peeps not been out there, things could have ended real ugly." Roe scolded.

"I'm just tired of niggas thinking I'm your lame side kick. I've been down with HPC since its birth and still don't get half the respect the streets show y'all."

"Niggas gon think what they wanna think. You just gotta do you."

"Already on it fam. Just wait until word really gets out about how I slumped over one of Junior's partners and took his ride after dropping you off," Chris announced proudly.

"I can see now you're just ignorant and gonna have to learn the hard way. Let's just hope it ain't your last lesson."

"Whatever. I'm fend to hit up Johnny's and get a burger with a fried ice cream honey bun."

"What the hell is you on? This car is as hot as Michael Jackson running a daycare and you thinking about eating!" Roe exploded, and then shook his head as he took notice of the small blood splatters in the interior.

"We fend to handle this right now. My prints are on the car!" he yelled.

"Chill mane. Po-Po ain't that good."

"That's exactly how stupid niggas get caught... over some dumb stuff!"

"Alright man," Chris conceded, pulling into the Touchless Automatic car wash on 10th St. He strode to the rear seats and began to clean out evidence before they dumped and burned the car that Chris had been driving in since the night before on stolen credit cards.

Looking over his shoulder, Roe glanced at him, "Mane, where the rags at? I'm gonna wipe down the front."

Chris was in the process of tossing old Wendy's bags and bottles from the back. "I think there are some towels in the trunk."

Roe opened the front door, pulled the keys out of

the ignition and took them to the trunk. He opened it and stared for several moments. Then he glanced up, "Chris." Busy cleaning the car, Chris didn't hear him. Roe looked around the empty car wash lot and called him once again, only louder, "Chris!"

Chris stopped cleaning and stuck his head out of the car, "What now?"

Roe motioned, "Come here." He lowered the trunk. Annoyed, Roe stepped out from the rear of the car.

"What?"

Angry, Roe gritted his teeth. "Get the hell over here now!"

Chris dropped what he was doing and hastily stepped to the back of the trunk where Roe stood. Roe looked around before he lifted the trunk again. "What the hell is that?" Looking inside the trunk, Chris displayed a surprised expression. "What the hell is a body doing inside the trunk?"

Lost for words, Chris shrugged. "Mane, I don't know I musta forgot about him."

"Nigga... how the hell you forget you riding around with a dead body in the trunk?" He grew even angrier when he remembered the hit Chris had picked him up to complete. "Nigga you had me riding in this

126

piece while we were supposed to roll up on some fools."
Pissed off beyond control he slammed the trunk hard.
Knowing that if anything had gone wrong he could have
been doing life behind some petty nonsense, Roe wiped
down the front as he continued to curse aloud at Chris'
stupidity, "Trying to get me caught in your mess. You're
on your own," Roe said as he stormed from the parking
lot on foot before he did something he might regret like
putting a bullet in him.

With the severity of the situation finally dawning
on him, Chris drove out to Dover to dispose of the
corpse.

On the way back into town, Chris lit up a blunt to
relieve the tension. This was the first time he had to
handle something of this magnitude solo. His nerves
were on edge.

As the relaxing smoke filled his lungs and took his
mind to a different realm, his foot unknowingly got
heavy on the pedal bringing his speed to ten over the
limit. Just as he crossed into city limits, an idle state
trooper clocked him whizzing by and consequently
turned on his sirens and gave chase.

"Shoot!" Chris said noticing the flashing lights in
the rear view mirror as he flicked the roach out the
passenger side window and attempted to air out the car
before pulling to the side of the highway.

"License and registration," the trooper requested in a curt tone.

After passing the officer the license and registration he found in the glove compartment, he waited nervously while he took the information back to his squad car.

Moments later the officer returned to his window, "Sir, Can you please step out the car."

"What's the problem officer?" Chris asked trying to mask his anxiety.

"I need you to step out the vehicle and place your hands on the hood. Do you have anything on you that I should know about?" he asked in a knowing tone.

"No."

"Are you aware that not only were you speeding, but your tags are expired?" the officer stated as he patted Chris down.

"No, it must have slipped my mind."

"So, is this your vehicle sir?" he asked inquisitively.

"No, a friend let me borrow it," Chris responded, trying to be quick on his toes.

"Do you mind if I search the vehicle?" the officer asked as a courtesy.

"Ordinarily I wouldn't mind, but with this being my friend's car, it wouldn't be right for me to let someone go through his things."

"So your friend who owns this car is a he huh?" the officer asked, reeling him in as he slid his handcuffs out of his holster. "And what's this friend's name?"

"Ugh... I forgot his real name, but he goes by Peanut," Chris said while cursing inwardly for not paying attention to the name on the registration.

"And how old is this Peanut?"

"I don't know, between 24 and 27, I guess," he said growing tired of this cat and mouse game.

"That's real interesting. I would love to hear more of this story down at the precinct," he said, slapping the cuffs on him.

"Hold up." Chris attempted to protest as another squad car pulled up. "I didn't do anything."

"Sir, please come with me," the officer said firmly guiding Chris into the back seat of his patrol car. Then he walked over to his fellow officer and briefed him on the situation followed by a quick search of the vehicle, which yielded a .9- millimeter.

Smugly striding back to the car and opening the back door, Officer Szczerbiak triumphantly held up the pistol. "And the plot thickens. I'm sure you'll be able to put together an interesting tale downtown to explain a loaded firearm being transported in a stolen vehicle."

Chapter 11

Chris fumed in the bullpen as he paced the floor, nervously waiting to appear before the judge for his arraignment. He had already used his one phone to call Donovan on his cell, but he never answered. Having been locked down for what felt like a lifetime, now he was pissed that a public defender was about to represent him. As he was being escorted before Judge Grimes with his lawyer beside him, the double door suddenly opened as Kevin Kennedy appeared in a sharp Armani suit walking confidently toward his lawyer. After a brief discussion, Chris' public defender handed his paperwork over to Mr. Kennedy.

In a Cochran type fashion Kevin got his charges reduced and bail lowered to $2,500. After Chris was bailed out, he stood in front of the courthouse; shaking hands with his lawyer then watched him walk off.

Ripping open his property bag he sifted through his personal effects and cursed when he discovered his cell phone battery was dead. As he scanned the area for a pay phone, a blue Cadillac with dark tinted windows pulled up and honked its horn. Cautiously eying the vehicle as the rear window began to descend, he grew nervous when he recognized Dee.

"Relax mane, I just need to get at you for a sec," Dee called out.

"I'm good. My peeps are on the way," Chris responded.

"Is that any way to treat the nigga that sent you the lawyer and paid your bail?" Dee asked as confusion etched across Chris' face. "Now get in the car. We need to talk."

Reluctantly, Chris got in the back seat with Dee. As the driver pulled off he couldn't help but wonder what happened to HPC looking out for fam and not answering his call. He had even left a message on Donovan's cell phone to come down and handle business.

Picking up his perplexed vibe Dee said, "Look, I ain't trying to tell you what to do, but I recognize a true soldier when I see one. With that being said, you should start thinking about what is best for you and you only. It's the only way to succeed in this game." Dee paused and watched Chris. He was a master of mind games and deceit, and played on people's emotions and greed to use them to his advantage. He was planting the seed in Chris' mind and would wait for it to patiently grow. "If your own people ain't with you, that means they're against you or are using you as a pawn. You already know had I not come through, that pretender of a lawyer you had would have had you still rocking that county jump suit," Dee added.

"Not to appear ungrateful, but I got the feeling that your motives involve pimping me out as a pawn on your team," Chris said timidly.

"I just can't figure why you ain't playing a bigger role in your operations or running your own. You supposed to be able to pay your own bail and be making millions, but instead you barely have two nickels to rub together."

Pulling up in the Parkview Hotel parking lot, the driver cut the engine.

"What are we doing here?" Chris asked.

"Well, that all depends on what you have to tell me... now before you start playing quiet mouse, consider your options." Producing two room keys from his pocket he held one in the palm of each hand while the driver turned to face him with a pearl handled chrome .9 cocked and ready to bust. "This key opens door number one which contains two of Clarksville's baddest hoes, ready to give in to your every desire... whereas this key opens door number two which contains two of Clarksville's most vicious killers, ready to set your remains on fire... the choice is yours."

"What do you want to know?" Chris said with defeat in his voice.

"See, I knew you had smarts... for starters where has Tee been hiding Ariana?"

"Don't get me lying on that one," Chris replied, followed by the driver raising the .9 at his head. "I'm for real. All I know is they got into a heated argument one day and she left him."

"I really find it hard to believe she would just leave him without a trace. Coast, do this nigga and tell the clean-up boys upstairs to take care of the mess."

"Wait! I promise, I don't know anything about her whereabouts, but I can give you something else."

Holding his hand up to signal for East Coast to slow his roll, "This better be worth my while or I'll make sure your death is slow and painful," he threatened.

"I know you got a personal vendetta against Tee and everyone he is close to. Well, as you may or may not know, his right hand man Donovan has been trying to keep his wifey low key."

"Oh, really?" Dee said, intrigued with his mind pondering devious ways to get at Tee through Donovan's pain. "So how would I meet this rare gem that was able to tame Mr. Lady's Man?"

"Her name is Naomi and I think she still works at Convergys," he answered.

"You've done well," Dee said tossing the key to door number one to Chris. "Enjoy the beauties upstairs and for your safety I recommend we keep this between us."

As Chris exited the vehicle and walked towards the stairs, he couldn't help but feel like Judas in the flesh. Little did he realize as he opened the door to his paradise filled room that Lashay, who came out of her room to call up Brittany so that her trick for the day wouldn't be all up in her business, saw the whole transaction.

"Girl, something just ain't right about that," Lashay said trying to put two and two together.

"What is it? Was he just another wanna be stunting hard or was the dick just that good?" Brittany asked, ready to live vicariously through the details of Lashay's explicit sex life.

"Who's Jonathon? Please, that was one of the quickest $100 I've ever earned. If it was an Olympic event he would have taken home the bronze medal, if not the silver, for breaking the under a minute record."

"Dang, I figured he would have been able to back all that talk up with his fine Panamanian features," Brittany said, wishing the guys she found attractive found her desirable.

"The only thing he didn't lie about was his head game being vicious. I swear that tongue of his could have swum the Panama Canal and back again with the way he was lapping away at my wetness."

"Nasty trick," Brittany said playfully.

"Whatever. Just because you wanna be me don't mean you gotta hate the game," Lashay shot back jokingly.

With the watered down truth of the matter assaulting her head on, Brittany changed the subject. "So what wasn't right earlier?"

Thinking back to what she had just witnessed, "I'm not sure what to make of what I just saw... can you think of why Chris would be getting out of a car with Dee?"

"Are you sure it was Dee?"

"I'm positive. I'd recognize that cocky no good nigga anywhere. He actually had the nerve to roll down his window and wink at me."

"Now that's just triflin. Maybe they arranged a truce," Brittany said, trying to make sense of things.

"I don't even know the whole story, but with the bad blood between him and Tee, I don't see that happening. Plus you already know they wouldn't send Chris to represent for HPC in a treaty."

"Unless he was working out a side deal under the

table," Brittany offered.

"I wouldn't put it past him. After all it was his girl that got Tony shot up."

"Girl you need to tell Tee before something else pops off."

"Forget Tee. After the way he dogged Ariana, I could care less what happens to his trifling behind!"

"I agree what he did was messed up, but you know as well as I do that it would hurt Ariana deeply if anything were to happen to him."

"He's a big boy, so I'm sure he can manage. Now if you want to warn that nigga, go right ahead, but like I said I could care less."

"Fine!" Brittany said hanging up the phone. She immediately called Tee to fill him in.

"Are you sure?"

"Yeah, Lashay witnessed it with her own eyes," Brittany said. "She would have told you herself, but still hasn't gotten over the way you and Ariana split ways."

"I appreciate you giving me a heads up. Speaking of Ariana, have you talked to her lately?" Tavares asked.

"We talk from time to time."

"Where has she been holding up and how has she been?" Tee asked, trying to mask the concern in his voice and sound nonchalant.

"Last time we talked she was staying with her aunt in South Carolina and is doing just fine. In spite of things, I think she still misses you somewhat. She does seem a little distant though."

"Hey I gotta run. Thanks for the tip. I'll shoot you a little something for your trouble."

"You know, ordinarily I would have turned you down, but with these high gas prices, I'll take you up on your offer."

"Bet, and if you don't mind, can you ensure Ariana gets a nice cut?"

"Why don't you call her and send it yourself?"

"Now just ain't the time for us to pick up convo again, plus I know she probably wouldn't accept the money if she knew it was from me. I'll send more than enough to hold you over for a while, just make sure Ariana is strait."

"Okay."

Chapter 12

The next day the sun refused to show itself and grace the streets with its warm glow. With the sky hidden by heavy clouds rolling across it, the clouds were a mixture of grays ranging from light hazy gray to a heavy dark smoggish gray that cast its dreadful shadow over the world beneath it.

Inside the detail shop, Tee found himself caught up in another early afternoon meeting. This time, however, with him being the chairman who organized it, he was ready to deal with the issue at hand.

With Donovan, Roe, and Vince in attendance, Tee called the meeting to order. "Last night I heard some very disturbing news," Tee said, pausing to make sure he had everyone's attention. "Before I let the cat out of the bag, who was the last person to see Chris?"

As everyone glanced around the room at each other trying to recall their last interaction with Chris, Roe chimed in, "I got into a riff with dude about 2 weeks ago over some hot boy stunt he pulled."

"What went down?" Tee inquired.

"I figured the reason Chris fell off the map was because he bit off more than he could chew and was trying to lie low," Roe said after briefly recapping two days' worth of drama filled events.

"Now that I think about it, he may have gotten locked up," Donovan added.

"What makes you think that?" Vince asked.

"Around the time Chris was going through that drama, someone left me a message begging me to bail them out of jail. They sounded so shaken up that I could barely make out what they were saying," Donovan replied.

"Tee, obviously you know something that we don't. So let's get on with it," Roe said, growing impatient.

"Well, like I said earlier, I got a call last night about someone seeing Chris casually get out of a car with Dee and stroll into a hotel room."

"What are you getting at?" Vince asked attempting to piece the puzzle together.

"If what Donovan described was really Chris calling him about bail, and he got locked up behind any of that drama with Roe, then how else would he have gotten out within two weeks?" Tee replied.

"That does sound a little suspect," Donovan said.

"Suspect! With that nigga its way past suspect. He

140

fits the description to a 'T',' Roe added.

"My thoughts exactly. The question now is how do we proceed?" Tee said looking around the room.

"I don't know about y'all, but it's over once I catch up to him," Roe threatened.

"Believe me, we're with you fam, but until we take care of loose ends, our operations are vulnerable," Tee explained.

"Yeah, he does know about a lot of our inner workings," Donovan said.

"So, what we need to do is switch things up and hurry up and clap that nigga," Vince concluded.

"Naw, screw that! I want every nigga involved to taste my lead," Roe said.

"To make that happen we gon have to get that scary nigga to give up names," Vince replied.

"With your reputation for torture, that shouldn't be a problem," Tee said locking eyes with Roe.

"Aiight, so Tee, if you're through using the Oak Grove cut, I suggest we move home base there and just play it by ear," Donovan proposed.

"You got it," Tee nodded in approval.

"Now that's settled. I gots streets to sweep. Holla at me as soon as the coward turns up on the radar," Roe said, rising to his feet and heading for the door with Vince close on his heels.

"Mane, I'm glad that nigga Roe is on our side," Donovan said.

"You and me both," Tee replied.

{{{{{{{{{{{{{{{{{}}}}}}}}}}}}}}}}}

Later that evening, Naomi couldn't help but feel like she was walking on sunshine, even on a cloudy day. Although Donovan didn't return her confession of love, she respected him for not just telling her what she wanted to hear and genuinely caring about her. As far as her professional life, keeping her attendance right and meeting all the performance and quality metrics finally paid off. She got the new supervisor position and was getting used to her new hours working the night shift.

At Convergys, finding decent parking during the peak daytime was next to impossible. She had to park so far in the back that she could have almost been confused for a Waffle House customer had their parking lot not been deserted. Making matters worse, rain was pouring down and she had left her umbrella at home. As she rounded the first corner towards the back lot, lightning flashed, thunder boomed, and the skies roared.

With her head down, she battled the elements and hurried toward her car without noticing the blue mini van parked next to her on the driver's side with the windows blacked out. As she fumbled with her keys, the van doors exploded open with two masked men snatching her up before she could let out a scream for help.

"Shut the hell up trick!" barked the stockier of the two with a gruff voice as he slapped her face causing her head to crash into the backside window.

"I don't have any cash on me, but you can have my debit cards," she whined.

"Didn't my boy tell you to shut up? What part of that don't your simple behind understand?" the leaner one asked, with his long slender hands wrapped around her throat as he pushed her on the back seat.

Meanwhile his partner closed the side doors and locked them. "Let's make moves!" the stockier one called out to the driver.

"Please...Please don't do this," she pleaded. "If its money you want, I can have a friend make arrangements to get that for you."

"Trick please. This is one debt that you don't have the means to pay," the lean one said as he continued to

143

choke her while his eyes traveled the length of her body lingering on the areas he found fascinating. Seeing the cruel intentions in his eyes she could only imagine what horrors awaited.

"Hurry up mane, I've been wanting to shove this dick in her since I saw her up in Kickers trying to act all sadiddy," the stockier one said while stroking his manhood through his jeans.

With his focus diverted to his partner, Naomi used that opening to wildly knee him in the groin causing him to double over in excruciating pain. Seeing a brief light at the end of the tunnel she climbed over the back seat and reached for the handle only to have the stocky one grab her by the back of her neck and slam her down on the seat.

"You know what hoe? At first I thought about gagging you, but now I'm fend to make you squeal like a pig for making this difficult."

Ripping her damp blouse to expose her sensual C-cups, he called for his partner to hold her down while he undressed her. Once naked, the leaner one held her face down on the back seat by pushing her arms behind her back police style while his boy rammed his erection deep inside her pussy with urgency. Gritting her teeth, she refused to give him the satisfaction of screaming out until he used the forced dampness from him pounding away to callously enter her butthole causing her to wail

144

out as she felt her skin rip and blood start to ooze out as tears streamed down her face.

For the next three hours the three of them took turns violating her over and over until they were good and exhausted. Having completed their mission, they pulled back into the Two Rivers Mall parking lot and threw Naomi, who had passed out, into the backseat of her own car and drove off.

{{{{{{{{{{{{{{{0}}}}}}}}}}}}}}}

The next morning, Tee's peaceful slumber was interrupted abruptly by his phone. Hesitantly picking it up from the built in shelf in the headboard, he quickly answered once he saw it was Donovan. "I hope the only reason you're calling me before the crack of dawn is to tell me y'all found Chris."

"If only that were the case," Donovan growled through clenched teeth. "Them coward niggaz came after Naomi."

"What you mean came after her?" Tee asked groggily for clarification.

"Mane, they kidnapped her from her job and raped her. Then they left her unconscious in her car. Some Good Samaritan noticed the dome light still on in the car because the door wasn't shut good and discovered her laid out in the back seat bruised up with her clothes torn.

145

Once he got her to come to, he called the cops who after taking statements took her to Gateway Medical Center."

"I just got to the hospital about 10 minutes ago. I swear when I get my hands on that nigga, he'll wish he never knew what HPC stands for."

"Focus on being there for Naomi right now. I'll take care of putting the price tag on that nigga," Tee said reassuringly.

"Aiight fam," Donovan said, then disconnected the line.

Several hours later, after spreading the news of the bounty, Tee found himself lounging in the back patio chair staring off into nowhere. As he casually sipped on a Long Island Iced tea and thanked God that Ariana was nowhere near harm's way, thoughts of their first time being intimate filled his mind:

With fresh dew still on the grass, and the wet glaze still on the house, Tee pulled up to a quiet house. All was calm; all but the birds still chirping and that fresh moist breeze as if it was blowing in off of a still lake.

As he slowly approached the house, he noticed that even inside the house was quiet. He was expected, wasn't he? Sure he was. He had just received a call that morning, along with directions, to come right in because the door would be unlocked. Okay, maybe she was

146

playing around.

Without any further thought, he reached out and grabbed the cold, moist doorknob and entered.

He called her name once, then twice, wondering where she could be. He slowly searched through the living room and into the kitchen. As he went into the kitchen, he took a peek onto the back porch. He noticed the breeze had calmed down a bit, but the birds were still singing their early morning orchestra. Just as a beautiful day should start.

As he broke from his gaze, he thought he heard a noise, but from where?

So, he began his playful search towards the bedrooms. He just knew she must be there; it was the last area of the house. He took a quick peek into her mother's room just to be sure; he didn't think she would be there. As he moved on towards her room, where surely she must be, he passed the bathroom, but heard nothing. What he did was feel warmth like a summer breeze reach out and fill his body from head to toe. As he thought maybe she retreated back to her room from a steamy hot shower, he could smell something so sweet; a quick flash of a garden full of fresh flowers was in his mind's eyes and lingered there for a moment.

After the hypnosis broke, he slowly crept towards her bedroom where he thought he would find his radiant queen lying upon her bed perhaps. What kind of clothing he would find her in, he wondered.

He slowly reached for the knob and turned it gently so as to not make any noise. In he went... nothing. It was as empty as all of the rest of the house, but that warmth spilling from the bathroom; it was so warm in his mind he said, "I have to go back. She is there."

As he turned around, he caught the scent of a sweet aroma. Its fragrance was that of a warm sweet vanilla sugar. As he approached the door and reached out for the knob, the warmth grew in him causing a tingle all the way down his spine.

With that fragrance enticing him, he opened the door with his eyes half open in caution of such brightness, and he was right for thinking that way. For what he saw when he entered the room, it all hit him at once. The warmth, the sweet fragrance, and Ariana; with her beautiful, bright brilliant face of light as if she were some kind of angel sent down from the heavens, resting her eloquent body atop the steamy, hot water. Her body, in all its silkiness, with the beautiful smooth edges of her face, just above the water, nearly lit up the whole room like the celestial light from the sun.

He carefully and quietly began to take off his shirt and walk over to her. She slid her hand around his waist, then up and around the back of his neck, then pulled him forward. As their lips slowly pressed together, their tongues twirling around and back and forth. As they kissed he slid his hand slowly from her shoulder down the silky curves of her breast, her nipples were already hard. From in between her full, vivacious breasts, his hand slid slower, further down the center to her belly button, where he stopped for a brief moment, twirling his fingers around in a very seductive way.

She was well ready, but he wasn't. He was still halfway dressed, so as he stood up, her hand slid down his chest to his pants and further. As he took as step back, he saw in her eyes, her searching, wanting, and needing so badly and he was going to give her exactly what she desired and some.

As he slid off the last of his clothes, she reached out for him. Taking her offer, she helped him into the steamy body of soothing water. When he caressed her body, it felt like satin and silk just sliding around so easily. He instantly wanted her just as bad or maybe even more.

The moaning and the deepness of their breathing went well into noon. Needless to say, the water never got cold that morning.

Chapter 13

Two states away, Ariana was just getting settled into the semi-rural area of Wedgefield, South Carolina.

Having left Clarksville about a month ago, she tried to keep herself busy to distract her thoughts from the only home she knew. Although she now lived in a doublewide mobile home with her Aunt Edith, she might as well have been staying there alone.

The distance factor from growing up without ever really seeing her aunt, much less carrying on a conversation carried over into many awkward silences.

From the outside looking in, one would have thought they were no more than roommates out of convenience who led two totally separate lives.

Only being in the fifth month of her pregnancy, she was still expected to maintain a job and pay for her living expenses. Luckily for her she left Walmart on good terms and was able to get a good reference for her to get rehired at the Super Center in Sumter.

As she glanced at her first pay stub, she warily shook her head at the meager wage. She knew it would be difficult to raise her child and eventually work towards moving out with the pay she would be bringing in.

So when Brittany called her up a week and a half ago about mailing her a money order, she initially wanted to decline out of pride, but had to reluctantly accept.

With today being her day off, she decided to keep busy by straightening up the living room and kitchen. Just as she was powering off the vacuum and preparing to roll up the chord, Edith walked in carrying a newspaper along with the mail.

"This just came in for you," she stated as she handed the envelope on top of the stack to Ariana then walked back into her room.

As she opened the envelope and glanced at the amount of the money order, her eyes widened in surprise. "This has got to be a mix up," she said to herself. Expecting to receive no more than a few hundred dollars, the $2,000 was more of a shock then a surprise. Picking up the phone she called Brittany to verify the amount.

"Hey girl, what's up?" Brittany cheerfully answered.

"I'm looking at this money order you sent and wanted to make sure there wasn't a mix up."

"No, the only mix up would be if it were sent to the wrong address."

"So you meant to send me $2,000? As much as I could use the money, I can't accept that much from you."

"Think nothing of it. It's not even really from me if you want to know the truth. I was just the messenger."

"So who in their right mind would...? You know what. Don't answer that. Tee put you up to it didn't he? Well you just tell that low down nigga where he can shove his guilty conscience blood money!" Ariana spat.

"Girl, listen. The way he ended things was real foul, but for some reason I really believe there is more to it than either of us knows. For now, just look at the money as a down payment on child support."

Weighing her options, Ariana conceded, "I guess there wouldn't be any harm in accepting it. Lord knows I need all the help I can get right now."

"Who knows, there may be some hope for y'all to reconcile your differences," Brittany said.

"Now you're really pushing it. Anyway, what have I missed?"

"Well let's see..." After filling Ariana in with the details she knew of and a few of the rumors that were floating around, she concluded, "So now there's a man hunt in the streets for Chris."

Disgusted, Ariana responded, "I remember Naomi from school. She was always quiet and kept to herself. I can't imagine why some sick bastard would attack her like that."

"I don't know how much truth to it there is, but from what I gather Dee may have been behind it pulling the strings."

"It wouldn't surprise me at all with the way his demented mind works. I'm just sorry that Naomi got caught in the middle of everything."

"Don't take this the wrong way, but I am kinda glad you're gone. Knowing the twisted things Dee is capable of, I'd hate to think about what could have happened to you." As if a light went off in her head, "Do you think that could have been the reason why Tee flipped all of a sudden?"

With images of their last interaction flashing through her mind, "It's possible... but if you could have only seen the intensity in his eyes. That day still haunts me. It was as if my world shattered."

"Are you capable of forgiving him?"

"Girl, I know you mean well, now just ain't the time to deal with those emotions. I appreciate you sending the money and checking up on me from time to time. I gotta go," she said then hurriedly disconnected the line before Brittany could get another word in.

{{{{{{{{{{{{{{{}}}}}}}}}}}}}}}

Meanwhile back in Clarksville...

"What's up old man?" Tee said answering his phone.

"Not too much other than you have really been on my heart and mind over the past few weeks. How have things been going for you?" Reverend Williamson asked.

"I can't complain too much. Just been trying to maintain."

"I noticed you haven't been by the house lately to visit with your mom. You know she really misses you."

"Yeah, I know it's been a while. Things have been kind of hectic."

"Son, I pray for you every day, especially when I see or read about all the violence plaguing our city on TV and in the newspaper. Now I ain't trying to preach to you, but I would like to lay eyes on you from time to time. Do you think we can do lunch today?"

"Can I get a rain check? I have a little running around to do today."

"Sure I understand... Maybe another time. Take care of yourself son."

"Will do... Oh, and pops."

"Yes, son?"

"Keep praying for me. One of these days it will pay off," he said before closing his flip phone.

Almost immediately his phone came to life with another incoming call. "What's good?" Tee answered after flipping it back open.

"You ready to ride?" Roe asked, more as a statement then a question.

"How far out are you?" Tee replied, as he inspected himself in the full length mirror to ensure his Taurus .45 didn't bulge out in his front pocket.

"Turning down your block as we speak."

"Alright, I'll be down in a minute."

After locking the side door, Tee walked the length of his driveway and entered Roe's Cutlass on the passenger side.

As Roe pulled off, Tee asked, "So what's the word on the street?" as he turned to Vince in the back seat and dapped him up.

"From what I hear he's been spotted a few times, but never long enough to get at him." Vince answered.

"Has anyone picked up on any trends?" Tee probed.

"Trends?" Vince questioned.

"Yeah trends, like who he is usually spotted with, where, and what days. Chris is pretty predictable. I bet there is a pattern."

"I wouldn't put it past him to still be chasing after Quanetta," Roe added.

"We got anybody keeping a tab on her?" Tee asked.

"We will before the day is over," Roe responded.

"Now that I think about it he's been sighted a few times on Austin Peay's main campus," Vince stated.

"Yeah he's probably using the campus as a means of slipping in and out of the Bricks," Roe said.

"Ain't Quanetta's spot just off of Lincoln Dr.?" Tee asked.

"Naw, she used to stay there, but is now even closer to the school off of Marion St.," Roe explained.

"Let's head over there. We might just get lucky."

"Aiight," Roe replied, as he turned left from New Providence Blvd. onto Kraft St.

After an uneventful drive through Lincoln Homes also known as Brick City, Roe dropped Tee back off at his house.

Once settled into his basement office, he set out to do his daily marketing for Phantom and his newly acquired music artist Antonio French. As the different Facebook profiles came and went they became just a blur to him with his mind drifting in and out of the past.

It began in the still of the night, the only time thoughts can be heard without any distractions the mind is able to work without being disturbed. While trying to figure out the hows and whys things happen the way they do. Searching and praying for answers that seem like they never come through. The million dollar question being, "Who am I" and "Why do I exist." Everyone has their own theory with their own special twist. Who to believe and who to trust? Why does it even matter, in the end ashes to ashes, dust to dust? What is really right and what is wrong? Why do people have to be something they're not just to belong? Weren't life, liberty, and the pursuit of happiness the American Dream? Why then do we get chastised for choosing not to be a part of society's political and analytical regime? Why are many called, but only few chosen? What made them worthy in the first place to be called by Him who chose them? But who is man to question the things of the Most High? Whenever He sees fit, He will reveal all the whats and whys.

As the remnants of the rhythm of the rhyme that inspired his enlightened poetic expressions while incarcerated flowed through him, all the drama in his life seemed irrelevant. With his spiritual eyes half open, he began to dial his parent's home number.

"Hello, Williamson's residence," his mom answered in a cheerful singsong tone.

"Hey ma it's me."

"You sure you got the right number? My son never calls here unless there is a problem. You're not locked up again are you?" she jokingly said with some sincere sarcasm.

"I see someone hasn't lost their sense of humor. Everything is cool this way. I was just tryin to catch up with Dad."

"You just missed him. He had to be in early so he could be prepared to preach tonight."

"Oh ok."

"Anything I can help you with?" she probed.

"Naw, not really. I was just trying to follow up with him."

"Well you know you could always meet him up there."

"It's been a while, but I might just swing through and surprise him."

"Really? That would mean so much to him," she said with that singsong creeping back into her voice. "Do you want me to save you a seat up front?"

"Naw, I think I'm just going to slide in on the side where I used to sit growing up."

"Okay, well I need to finish getting ready. I'll see you there."

"Alright, talk to you later."

"I know you aren't about to get off this phone without telling me you love me."

"Girl, you should already know you're my favorite mother."

"Boy please, I better be, considering I'm your only mother."

"And I love you for it."

"That's more like it. I love you, too," she said before disconnecting the line.

As Tee entered the front lobby of Faith Outreach Church and opened one side of the double doors leading into the sanctuary, he could feel the gazes of all the long time members watching him. Some of the more tenured ushers went out of their way to greet him and offer assistance with seating, but he kindly declined. Sure enough, things hadn't changed much. The teenagers still sat on the far left side of the church away from their watchful parents' eyes. Taking his seat among them, Tee acknowledged some of the familiar faces while the praise team set the atmosphere for the Word to be delivered.

After the last worship song came to a close and the offering was collected, Reverend Williamson took his position behind the pulpit.

"Praise the Lord Saints," Reverend Williamson proclaimed with the congregation faintly repeating after him. "I said praise the Lord Saints," he repeated with more fervor, causing the congregation to follow suit in unison."

"Now that's more like it. I was beginning to question your understanding of true praise. After the message that Pastor Vallejos preached about the power of praise, there shouldn't be a question in our minds to the importance of our willingness to praise God."

"Building off his message, true praise is a natural response from a heart that has been forgiven. Forgiveness is a necessary foundation for praise, and holds the key to our entire relationship with God."

"No one knows our nature better than God who made us. He knows we are disobedient, and our disobedience is what separates us from Him."

"He longs for restoration of our broken relationship. He knows He can't depend on us to do anything right. He decided a long time ago to depend on Himself instead. Our disobedience deserves death, so God let His own Son die for us. Thus, our debt is paid and God's system of forgiveness has been set up."

"Forgiveness means to give up ones claim to compensation from an offender. We are the offenders. Based on what Jesus has done, God gives up all claims of repayment from us. He holds nothing against us. It sounds so simple, but it's obvious that we don't fully understand it. If we did, we would be overwhelmed with gratitude and filled with joy for the rest of our lives. Most of us undervalue God's system of forgiveness. We can only be thankful that He doesn't."

"The plan of redemption is designed to restore our relationship with God; it doesn't work unless we accept it. One of the hardest things for us to admit is that we can't do anything right. We'll do almost anything to keep us from swallowing our pride and accepting what God has done for us. Part of the reason is that we have been taught from childhood to "do our share" and earn our way. We are proud to be self-made."

"Pride in our own accomplishments separates us from God. We want to handle things on our own, and we struggle along until our problems become unbearable. Even then, we try to resist God's solution and say, "I'd be ashamed to come to God like a beggar. I'll wait until I get myself out of this mess first.""

"Some of us try halfhearted confessions. We say we are sorry, but our actions deny our words and we go right back to doing what we did before. What is lacking in that type of repentance is surrendering to God's will. Surrender to give up oneself unto the power of another. To do anything less in our relationship with God is only to kid ourselves. It probably means we aren't really sorry for doing wrong, but only for getting caught."

"True forgiveness that restores our relationship with God depends on our surrender to His will. We can't have a close relationship with Him unless we are surrendering to Him completely."

"Our rejection of His forgiveness may not seem so

obvious. We may say we admit our wrongs and accept His forgiveness, but behave as if we are paying the penalty for our own sins. Many people in that category become Christian workers. They give their lives in service to God as pastors, Sunday school teachers, lay leaders, nuns, or priests, but they labor more out of a sense of duty than of love and know little joy in serving Christ. All of us at one time or another have behaved like that."

"We may look good in the eyes of others as we play the martyrs role, paying God what we feel we owe Him. But that isn't what He wants from us. We are refusing to give Christ credit for canceling our debts. We are rejecting Him as our Savior, and it is pride, not humility, that motivates us. David addressed himself to God saying, 'For You don't desire sacrifice, or else I would give it; You don't delight in burnt offerings. The sacrifices of God are a broken spirit. A broken and a contrite heart these O God, You won't despise.' Psalms 51:16, 17"

"It is a proud and unbroken heart that insists on paying for its own sins. Jesus said, 'Come to Me, all of you who labor and are heavy laden, and I will give you rest,' Matthew 11:28. There is no heavier burden in this world than trying to carry the penalty for our own sins. As long as we do that we will never know God's forgiveness. We will never know the joy of a cleansed heart and our relationship with God can never be a close one."

164

"A tremendous load will roll off our backs when we learn to accept God's forgiveness completely. Our need for it shouldn't be a source of despair, but of rejoicing. Only a heart that has been forgiven understands the love of God. The more we are forgiven the more we love Him and the more we are able to praise Him. Then we can sing like David, 'What happiness for those whose guilt has been forgiven! What joy when sins are covered over? I want relief for those who have confessed their sins and God has cleared their record... So rejoice in Him, all those who are His, and shout for joy, all those who try to obey Him,' Psalms 32:1-2, 11."

As Reverend Williamson closed his Bible and notes, the pianist played a very soft chord in the background while he tilted his head back and seemed to be peering into the Heavens for direction on what to speak next. When his head leveled back to face the congregation, a pained expression replaced the confident one that was on display moments ago.

"While some of you have heard parts of my testimony, there are others who may not know how far I've come because of God's grace and mercy. At one point I fell victim to drugs and destructive vices that I eventually got caught up in. I can remember being around the age of 20 to 22, confused, ready to give up and throw the towel in. I tried everything and nothing could satisfy me. Couldn't get peace. I thought that if I could get the money I would be good. I had a car with big rims."

"It was a 1974 Monte Carlo, jacked up with the speaker system blasting. Everybody in the neighborhood saying 'look at him go,' but I was just miserable because it was all temporary. It took some time before I just flat out got tired of the sin. It just wasn't fun anymore. So when I got back to the barracks one day I threw away my last joint... Okay, well I told the truth before so I'm going to tell the truth now. I sold my last joint for $1 praise God. I just couldn't let it go. I sold that last one, but that was it. I cut everything loose, but at the same time, I really didn't know where I was going from there. I really wasn't looking for God. I was just tired of that lifestyle. And by me coming to that realization, I believe God spoke to my motor pool sergeant who invited me to church. Had he tried to invite me a month earlier I would have probably laughed in his face, but of course God's divine timing caught me when my heart was tender and broken. Although I didn't give my life to the Lord that first Sunday, I continued to come back week after week until I asked Jesus into my life and accepted his forgiveness for all my wrong doings. Let me tell you even though things in my life didn't necessarily all change for the better overnight, a huge burden fell off my shoulders. For the first time, I actually felt hope and was optimistic about my future."

As Tavares' father continued to explain his heart felt conversion to the congregation, Tee felt a stirring within his own heart and spirit. Before he knew it he was standing on his feet with some of the other members of the church that were moved as well. Almost on autopilot he reached into his jacket pocket and pulled out a single black glove and made his way to the pulpit. Tuning out all those in attendance, with each step towards his father he felt the weight burdening his shoulders begin to slide off.

When Reverend Williamson took notice of his son approaching he let out a shout for joy and quickly reached out to embrace him. Before he could wrap his arms fully around him Tee placed the balled up glove in his hand as tears began to stream down his cheeks. Unsure of what the glove meant, Reverend Williamson pocketed it and allowed tears of joy to run down his cheeks as well.

As the congregation witnessed the scene, most of the tenured members understood it to be the Prodigal Son coming home. The sanctuary erupted into a joyous outburst. As the jubilation became contagious, everyone stood to their feet and began to give God the glory.

When the praise began to die down, Reverend Williamson began to regain his composure. "All praise be to God for bringing my son home. For those of you out there who may be on the verge of losing hope on your wayward children..... I want to declare to you that if you rear up a child in the way he should go and when he is old he will not depart from the path. God's Word will not return back void," he said, raising Tavares hand in the air triumphantly, which produced another round of praise.

167

"Son, would you like to say something to the church?" Reverend Williamson asked.

Taking the cordless mic offered by one of the deacons, Tee replied, "I still have a ways to go to get to where I need to be spiritually. Tonight the scales were removed from my eyes, enabling me to see the right path. I will need the grace of God to sustain me as I walk upright in His direction. I just want to ask you all to keep me uplifted in your prayers."

After a brief applause, Reverend Williamson closed out the service with prayer only to have a long line of members linger around more than usual to shake his hand and hug Tee with words of encouragement. As the crowd thinned out, Reverend Williamson pulled Tee to the side and arranged for them to meet up in the lobby at Arby's.

Having waited in a booth for 20 minutes, Tee contemplated ordering something just to pass the time. Just as the fresh aroma of roast beef began to pull him to the counter, Reverend Williamson walked in and sat across from him.

"I'm curious son. What happened that brought you back to church?" Reverend Williamson asked.

"I guess you can say I am finally growing so tired of that lifestyle that I desperately need a change in my life. Even in the midst of darkness, I can see that faint light of hope at the end of the tunnel," Tee answered.

"I'm happy to hear it. So what was the significance behind the glove and why do you have medicine balled up in the finger tips?"

"For someone who used to be into dealing drugs, you really don't have a clue what those are?" Seeing the confused look on his father's face, he continued, "The different colored pills are called ecstasy and as for the significance of the glove let's just say it kept my trigger finger warm."

"Boy, you have me riding around with drugs in the car. Now how would that have looked if I got pulled over with that?"

"I figured you would have recognized the pills for what they were and disposed of them at the church. You know how money driven I am. The street value in all that is over $300. I wanted to show you how sincere I was about being done with that nonsense."

"I'm glad to hear it. Now, if you'll excuse me I am going to take care of this," Reverend Williamson said as he rose to his feet and headed to the bathroom.

"Feel better now Mr. Paranoid," Tee said upon his return.

"Much better. So what will you do now that

you're flying straight to provide for your family?"

"The only thing I can do at this point, which is whatever it takes to make money the legit way. I got a friend that's gonna get me hired on with Washington Inventory and I got the music promotions on the side that is starting to pick up."

"I'll be sure to keep that in my prayers. If you need anything please don't hesitate to call. As long as you are trying to make it the right way I don't mind helping you along until you get on your feet."

"Thanks. I appreciate you being in my corner and will do my best to make you and mom proud from here on out."

After the father and son duo caught up on old times, they shook hands and embraced one final time before going their separate ways.

Chapter 14

The parking lot to the Women Center was jam packed with cars as if it were secretly a department store with a special clearance sale. After several minutes, they found a spot and walked into the humble looking establishment.

Instead of somber look on the inside, the décor featured resilient maroon walls, with an intricate flowery mid border separating the bottom half with its pastel sparsely flowery theme that matched the border. Two TV's on opposite sides of the room entertained the patrons who like the waiting room weren't somber looking at all.

As a matter of fact, as they waited in line to sign in, several visitors were smiling and cracking jokes, which eased some of Naomi's apprehensiveness and tension. It had been a whole eight weeks since the incident, but to Naomi she could remember it as if it were yesterday.

"You know as much as I thought I would hate this baby growing inside me, I've started growing attached," she said to Donovan.

Not wanting to get into that emotional discussion, he zeroed in on a pimple on her check and began to squeeze.

"Ouch!" she exclaimed. "Leave my face alone."

"Man up. I've just about got it all out," he said, showing her the pus on his thumb. "Plus it ain't like I got nails anyway."

"That makes it hurt worse because you have to squeeze harder," she complained.

"Whatever. Just stay still," he said as he squeezed more pus out of the whitehead.

"Ugh! I Feel like I'm bleeding," she whined.

"They say blood makes the grass grow, but with that little trickle I doubt you could get a dandelion to sprout up."

"Just get me a tissue before I hurt you to the point you can grow a field of dreams."

Content, Donovan went to the bathroom and returned with some tissue to wipe up the light spec of blood. They continued to make small talk until it was time for her to sign in, then find a seat in the crowded waiting room.

With no two seats together available, Donovan offered Naomi the closest one to the door leading into the clinic while he took one in the middle.

After about 20 minutes of waiting while the nurse called out patients by their first name and last initial, she finally called out "Naomi B."

Within a few minutes she returned with a piece of gauze taped to her index finger. Taking a seat, she motioned for Donovan to fill the vacant seat next to her.

Looking at the half empty waiting room, he commented, "I figured the process would take a while, but from what I can see they approach it like an assembly line."

"Did you think that all they did here was abortions?" she questioned as he nodded yes.

"They handle other women's issues as well."

"I guess that makes sense," he thought to himself as he remembered the lighthearted atmosphere when they first walked in. Just then he noticed out of the corner of his eyes a white lady with a bleached blond ponytail fighting back the tears only to give in. The bald man with sleeved tattoos accompanying her seemed to offer no support as she dealt with her personal demons and wiped her tears away.

After another 30 minutes, they finally called Naomi back again with several other females. This time she was gone so long that Donovan fell asleep for an hour and a half with the only thing awakening him was the abrupt bounce his neck made when his hand slipped off his chin.

When he glanced around the deserted lobby he noticed only a handful of people were left. Curious as to how much longer the procedure would last, he approached the sliding glass window and gently tapped it to get the receptionist's attention.

"Excuse me miss, I'm here for Naomi Brandt and was wondering how long the process was going to take?"

"One moment," she said while flipping through the charts. "Her group just finished the class down stairs and will be up shortly to pay for the procedure. After that you're looking at about a couple more hours."

He thanked her and waited another 20 minutes or so for her to meet with the receptionist, at which point he made his way back up to the window.

"How much are we looking at?" he asked the receptionist.

"Well, with the IV sedation and the RhoGAM shot for her not having her blood type, it's going to be $600." Reaching into his pocket he pulled out a wad and peeled out the amount in $50 bills then handed it to the receptionist.

"Hey beautiful," he said, getting Naomi's

174

attention. "I'm gonna run down the street for a lil while, but I'll be back way before you're done."

"Okay," she replied with a distracted look on her face.

While Naomi was going through the final stages to prep her for the process, Donovan met up with Celeste to pick up a few things from the Opry Mills Mall.

Having accomplished his task, he thanked her and quickly returned to the Women's Center so that he would be there by the time the procedure was complete.

Just as he was about to doze off in the lobby again, the door to the back area opened and Naomi slowly walked into the lobby with her head down.

Wishing he could take the weight off her shoulders and absorb the physical and emotional pain she felt, Donovan quickly got up and wrapped his arms around her. "I'm here baby," he whispered in her ear. "Today is all about you. Let me know what you want right now and I'll make it happen," he said sincerely as he squeezed her tightly.

"Right now I just want to get out of here and get some rest," she replied.

Holding the front door open for her, Donovan escorted her to the car and drove off.

With her falling asleep shortly afterwards, they rode in silence. Donovan, alone with his thoughts, began to reminisce about his last visit to the Lake of the Ozarks.

For Tavares, these Labor Day weekend outings were an annual affair where he got to spend time with his family from Saint Louis on a lakeside resort. Each year they enjoyed spades, dominoes, swimming, go carts, basketball, and each other's company, as they took a break from their day to day to routine.

This particular trip marked a significant moment in Donovan's life. It would be the closest thing to a family reunion that he had ever experienced.

Apprehensiveness and excitement intermingled as he wondered if he would be accepted. The four-hour drive to St Louis went by relatively quick. They visited several of Tee's relatives throughout the city that wouldn't be in attendance at the resort before he would meet up with the rest of the family at his cousin Charles' house.

Having opted to remain in the car for the brief visits and trips to the nursing home, this would be his first interaction with the St Louis crowd. Pulling into the quiet subdivision, they turned onto Elmore St. then followed it into a cul-da-sac enclosed by colorful houses and manicured lawns. From the eight cars that filled one driveway and lined the streets, Donovan felt like all eyes would be on the stranger as they approached the group congregated on the front lawn.

To his surprise, they regarded him as a family member they just hadn't seen in a while. Some even to the point of swearing up and down he had been a part of a few childhood memories. Not wanting to give up that intimacy, he played along with Tee following suit.

Once all parties arrived, they headed to their vehicles and hit the highway as if they were a caravan on their way across the Oregon Trail. With excitement overpowering any feelings of apprehensiveness that lingered, the three hour drive to the Ozarks seemed to last a lifetime.

Just before he asked the infamous question, "Are we there yet?" that drivers dread hearing, the sign broadcasting the Lakes of the Ozarks appeared. Looking about the car in amazement, Donovan peered out of the window into the vastness of the lakes on both sides of the highway filled with sailboats and speedboats competing for the title of King of the Sea.

"Are we almost there yet?" Naomi asked breaking his train of thought and causing him to smile.

"Almost, we'll be passing through St. Louis soon and just have about another two and a half hours to go. Did you want to stop somewhere and take a break?" he asked.

"Well I am a little hungry and have always wanted to see the Arch."

Glancing at his watch he replied, "I could go for a little break myself. Let's check out the Arch, and then grab a bite."

"Okay" she replied.

After crossing the Martin Luther King Bridge overlooking the Mississippi River, they got off the ramp onto Memorial St., passing Edward Jones Dome and the Casino Queen Riverboat Gaming.

Once they parked in the sparsely populated lot, Donovan made it through the short line fairly quickly due to it not being a holiday weekend. Naomi was viewing the informational exhibit and photographs of the construction of the Arch before they boarded the tram on the North leg. While briefly glancing through the brochure, they traveled at four mph until they reached the top of the Arch and peered out the observation window, taking in the St. Louis skyline from above.

When the sight-seeing was over, they grabbed sandwiches and hit the road. Once again silence replaced the idle chatter of their side trip as they came upon Exit 248. Traveling the length of Route 54, they eventually began to pass many tourist specialty shops, local restaurants, and the Osage Beach Premium Outlets, which boasted over 120 stores. Golf courses, watercraft stores, and high-rise lakeside resorts littered the area.

As they passed over the Lake Rd. Bridge, it was almost like deja vu for Donovan, with the various watercrafts roaming the lake in packs on a quest to conquer every square inch of its surface.

Shortly after crossing the bridge he turned left onto Winn Rd. and followed the winding road past the beautiful Villa Condominiums until they reached the lakeside Kapilana Condos.

Parking near the office, Donovan went inside to check in and returned with their keys. They drove the short distance and parked in front of building 10.

"Who are you supposed to be meeting?" Naomi asked sarcastically while Donovan exited the vehicle. "I don't feel like being around any of your business associates so please make it brief. I'll be waiting in the car."

"If you're done making an assumer out of yourself, would you care to join me for a weekend of peace and quiet?" he asked, with a slight bow as he opened her door.

"I can't believe you planned all this," she replied in disbelief. "Wait. You said the weekend. I don't have a change of clothes much less a toothbrush."

"Baby, you're worrying about the wrong things right now. Your girl Celeste helped me pick out a few items for you," he said, gesturing to all the bags in the backseat and cargo area.

Taking his extended hand, Naomi stood up and wrapped her arms around him, "Thank you, baby."

"Don't thank me just yet. You haven't even seen the room or the great view of the lakes."

"What are we waiting for?" she asked, snatching her copy of the key. "When you're finished bringing in the luggage, I need you to pour me a cold glass of water."

"Anything else Master?" he joked.

"I'll let you know when the thought crosses my mind. Until then you can count on doing a whole lot of cuddling."

While Donovan unloaded the car, Naomi toured the luxurious condo. She began with a brief walk through the modern kitchen and dining room that led to a huge living room with oversized couches that matched the décor. Next to the black leather recliner was a grand fireplace with a big screen TV adjacent to it. Wanting to see the rest of the house before venturing out the back door, she retraced her steps and turned right into the hallway. Behind door number one on the right was the main bathroom with a beach/ocean theme and to the left was a laundry that included a washer, dryer, and cleaning supplies. As she continued she saw a nice sized bedroom and to the right of it was the master bedroom. The first thing her eyes took in while opening the door to the master bedroom was the plush grand bed that she literally had to jump up to get on. Directly across from the foot of the bed was a sliding glass door that led to their private balcony overlooking the beautiful lake.

As Naomi leaned against the rail with the cool gentle breeze whispering across her skin, Donovan crept up and embraced her from behind causing her to flinch and jerk away in fright.

Confused, Donovan asked, "What's wrong? I thought you wanted us to be close."

Hesitantly she replied with pain and sorrow etched in her once cheery eyes. "As much as I want to put that dreadful night behind me, those memories still haunt me in my sleep... I just don't know if I'll ever be able to get used to a man's unexpected touch."

"We'll get through this together," Donovan said understandingly as he slowly stretched his hand towards her.

Tentatively matching his pace until their hands met and fingers interlocked, she mouthed a "Thank you" while quickly wiping a stray tear that attempted to slide down her face.

With the sun preparing to set for the evening and give way to the starry sky, she began to envision the day when her pain and sorrow would fade into the darkness and give way to a brighter tomorrow.

Chapter 15

The black sedan cruised down 9th St., then slowed and went in reverse with the window cracked confirming they had found who they were looking for. "There that nigga go right there. Let me out here and drive around the other side of the block to cut him off," Roe told Vince.

As Chris stubbed out his black and mild cigar to save it for later, he noticed a lone hooded figure approaching. Still buzzing from the 2 cans of 211 he consumed not even five minutes ago, he didn't even recognize the familiar characteristics of the figure until he was almost on him.

"Oh shoot!" Chris exclaimed, dropping the remnants of his 211, turning and running down Carpenter St.

"Don't make this harder than it's got to be!" Roe shouted as he charged after him.

Just as Chris was approaching the intersection where Ford St. would have given him access to Bailey St. so he could have made it back on main campus, the black sedan came to a screeching halt in front of him, causing him to slip on loose gravel to avoid running straight into the car.

Before he could recover, Roe pounced on him.

"Awe come on, fam... I ain't talk to nobody... it wasn't me, I swear!" Chris pleaded.

Roe pulled him up from the ground by his collar as his menacing eyes made Chris sweat.

"This is messed up. We all grew up together...why y'all doing this to me... it wasn't my fault. I didn't know she was working undercover for Dee. Plus they threatened to do me in on the spot." Unable to get Roe to hear his plea, he tried a different angle. "Let me make it right."

"And how do you propose to do that?" Roe asked.

With a glimpse of hope he replied, "I followed Quanetta to one of Kebo's stash spots one day to see if she was creeping on me. Matter fact not too long ago I seen him pick her up. They are more than likely there now."

"What does Kebo have to do with anything? Dee was the one that coordinated everything," Roe questioned.

"True, but Kebo was the muscle behind the hit."

"And how you figure that out Sherlock?"

"Because the day I followed Quanetta there, I had parked down the street and seen Dee leave shortly

184

afterwards."

"Hey, Roe, this is getting hot... handle that ish mane!" Vince called out.

"Hold on. I think we came up on some valuable information. Call the cavalry and tell them it's time... come on nigga lets go for a ride... and for your sake you better be telling the truth."

Chris smiled inwardly as he led them to Lucas Lane. Just as he predicted, Kebo's Expedition was parked out front. "There it is right there," he said pulling out his .44 and pushing the barrel against his temple, "You know if this turns out to be a trap or any info you gave us turns out to be proven wrong, I will find your lame behind and murk your mother in front of you before leaving you in the gutter like the filthy dog you are," Roe threatened.

With that inner smile evaporating, replaced by terror he attempted to reassure him, "I swear on everything that I love. I would never intentionally betray y'all. We like fam."

Knowing Chris wasn't stupid enough to cross him with his life on the line, they drove around the block to wait for Donovan and Tee to arrive. When they pulled up in a beige Acura Legend, Roe began to exit the sedan and got in the back seat.

"Junior?" Roe asked, with a confused expression on his face as he discovered Junior was behind the wheel instead of Tee along with his younger brother Troy in the back next to him.

"It's a long story, but Tee is gonna sit this one out. Junior was kind enough to fill in since he has some unfinished business with Chris," Donovan said.

Seeing Junior's trademark smirk through the rearview mirror, he already knew what time it was.

"Make sure it's slow and painful," Roe said to Junior prior to opening the door and walking back to the sedan with Donovan following suit.

"Get out!" Roe said to Chris as he snatched the door open.

"Hold up Roe. We straight now right?" Chris asked.

"Yeah, we straight... Tee is gonna take you by the new spot while we take care of these clowns."

Feeling at ease knowing Tee was one of the more levelheaded members from the Hollow Point, he hopped straight into the passenger seat without looking.

By the time he realized it was Junior driving it was too late. Troy smacked him upside the head with his firearm then dared him to make a move. Gulping down the sobs trying to escape his throat, Chris knew the end was near as Junior drove off.

Meanwhile, Quanetta was making good on one of her promises to deep throat Kebo and swallow all of his cum. As she served him lovely on her knees in one of the back rooms he got caught in the moment with both hands on her head thrusting her head in and out with rapid successions, "Yeah ma... right there... oh yeah... oh yeah... take that Ahhh!" A sudden loud crash at the door made them both stop cold. He quickly tucked his limp dick in his pants and pulled out his gat.

Easing toward the door he slowly turned the knob, but a volley of shots followed by loud screams and cries made him freeze in his tracks.

Quanetta watched petrified as he paced back and forth looking for a way out, but finding none with the windows bolted with master locks. More gunshots erupted followed by piercing screams causing her to cry out.

"Shut the hell up!" he hissed. Easing toward the door again he placed his ear against it. Hearing the footsteps grow louder and closer on the hard wood floors, he gripped the weapon tighter and closed his eyes. Deciding at that moment he wasn't going out like a chump, he looked toward the ceiling, mumbled a quick prayer and cocked the trigger.

187

Reading his expression, Quanetta knew what he would do next and frantically took cover underneath the bed with her eyes clinched tightly as she prayed profusely for a way out.

Suddenly he jerked the door open and started blasting. The noise was deafening as rapid flashes of gunfire lit up the hallway. Then just like that it was all over with his body crashing to the floor with a thud. When she opened her eyes she saw Kebo laid out in a pool of his own blood followed by a pair of black Airmax's that blocked her vision. Terror overcame her as someone ordered the back rooms to be searched. The shoes turned first and walked across the room to open and close the closet doors then returned. In one swift toss the mattress was flipped exposing her to the sawed-off shotgun being pointed at her by a masked man with maniacal piercing eyes. She knew it was over then and there as Roe unmasked himself.

"Roe wait! I'm sorry!" she pleaded to no avail.

"Yeah, you sorry alright, now wait for me in hell slut!" he said as he squeezed the trigger leaving her brain matter splattered against the wall.

Donovan and Vince entered the room with large bags filled with stacks of cash and hundreds of caps of bottled crack.

"Payback's a motha and now we're paid in full," Donovan said, holding up the bags in triumph. "Naw, there's still one more dish that needs to be served, but for now we need to vamp out before it gets hot in here."

As Donovan and Vince turned and ran out of the house, Roe stopped short at the door and looked down at Quanetta's corpse then up at the ceiling, "Tony, I told you fam, no one would touch one of us and go unpunished. Rest in Peace," he said before joining his partners.

Chapter 16

Hundreds of miles away, Ariana found herself seated across from a tall, barrel chested airman stationed at Shaw Air Force Base. Having seen each other a few times at the Walmart where she worked, Brandon finally got the nerve to approach her.

"Hey beautiful, how was your day?" he asked.

"Fine I guess, considering its only halfway over," she replied curtly as she prepared to clock out for a break in the back.

"Do you mind if I take up a moment of your time?"

"Yes, I do. I'm trying to go to lunch and feed my baby," while rubbing her barely showing belly.

Noticing her glowing face for the first time, he quickly shrugged it off. Having been to several duty stations and experienced the dating pool consisting of either women with kids, kids on the way, or planning on trapping a GI with kids, he actually preferred this scenario. At least this way there weren't already kids running around rampant that she would want him to play daddy to. Plus, with a bun in the oven he could hit it raw and leave it in without worrying about her trapping him.

That last thought brought a smile to his face as his eyes took in her pleasing sight. "Well in that case allow me the privilege of taking both of you out to eat," he proposed.

"Thanks, but I don't have much time to really go anywhere. I was just going to go get something from the Deli real quick," she said trying not to notice his cute dimples and well defined physique.

"There's a McDonald's right in here that we can hit up real quick which will get you your food faster than waiting in a regular line during this peak period," Brandon insisted as he pointed out the long lines at almost every register.

Sensing he wasn't going to take no for an answer, "Okay, let me get the crispy chicken meal," she conceded.

"That's more like it," he said triumphantly as he escorted her to the restaurant in the back.

As they enjoyed their meal and light conversation, Ariana began to feel more comfortable around Brandon. With her break coming to an end, she conceded more willingly this time and gave him her number before departing...

{{{{{{{{{{{{{{{}}}}}}}}}}}}}}}

Two days later, Tavares held court at his home. "So run this rumor by me that you stepping out the game?" Roe asked.

"Ain't no rumor to it. I've put in my fair share of work through the years and have paid many costs associated with it. I have reached a point in my life that if I don't end this cycle, I'm not only negatively impacting myself, but those around me that need me."

"What, you don't think HPC needs you in our corner? We supposed to be family," Roe said.

"We are, and I'm gonna always be pulling for y'all, but I have to think about my other family and my unborn son. Even though I didn't turn out perfect, I still had a father figure in my life who provided me with the tools I needed to make it in life. I refuse to continue to roll the dice of death or jail and run the risk of Ariana having to raise my son on her own."

"What about Dee? With all the stuff he masterminded, how can you let that ride?" Vince asked.

"I'll never be able to forget what he put me through... Never! At the same time, I understand that unless I can forgive him, I will never be able to move forward," Tee explained.

Before anyone else could speak to his last statement, Donovan interjected. "Look, I'm gon miss having you around, but I know the choice that you're making is the right one and wish that I had the courage and the will to do the same."

"The courage and will are there. That seed was planted years ago in your life. When the time is right it will bring forth fruit. In the meanwhile, I want y'all to know you all will remain in my prayers," Tee said.

"Okay, now that you've gone T.D. Jakes on us, there is still the matter of what to do with Dee. You already know once he regroups he will come back with a vengeance," Vince said.

"Let him come. It's about time we went head up anyway, Roe said, ready for action.

"That coward ain't fend to soldier up in the streets. He's just gonna put together another team of hitters and work behind the scene, Donovan added.

"Leave Dee to me," Tee said, causing all heads to turn into his directions in surprise. "The only way to get at him is to play his puppet master game."

"So what happened to all that Gandhi forgive and forget jazz you were talking about?" Roe asked.

"Enough people have been hurt behind a beef that really has nothing to do with them. Consider this my last deed for the team."

"You sure about this?" Donovan questioned.

"Yeah. The only thing I need for y'all to do is turn up the heat on sticking up his remaining stash spots, I'll handle the rest," Tee explained.

{{{{{{{{{{{{{{{}}}}}}}}}}}}}}}}}

A few weeks later Tavares pulled up in Kobe's Lock & Security Service, which was a well-respected establishment in the community for providing top rate home security for a fraction of the cost his competitors offered. Little did they know, Kobe's alias was B Durdy and his after hour's job was a safe cracking cat burglar.

As Tee entered the humble establishment the bells above the door chimed notifying Kobe he had customers.

"Well look what the streets dragged in," Kobe said dapping up Tee. "So what brings you by? Got a party planned and in need of supplies?" "Something like that... Can we chop it up in the back office?"

"Aiight, hold up and let me lock up," he said as he locked the door and turned the "Open"' sign around to indicate the store was closed.

"So what's good?"

"I'm in need of a favor."

"After the last one you did for me, you know I'm down."

"That's good to know, because this requires your special expertise."

"This must be a high stakes job."

"You could say that."

"Well get on with it. I can't close up shop all day for you to beat around the bush."

"Peep this. That nigga Dee done violated on so many levels that death ain't even befitting for him. I've already called in a favor from an old friend to dry up his operation for a while to make him vulnerable. Once a few other puzzle pieces fall in place, he'll be distracted. That's where you come in," Tee said, working out the details in his head as he spoke.

"I'm listening," Kobe responded, ready to hear what his role would be.

While Tavares went on to describe his plan, Kobe initially stared in disbelief until he had the complete picture laid out for him, causing him to smile at Tee's deviousness. "Ya know, I never would have thought you had it in ya, but like I said earlier I'm down."

"I knew I could count on you to have my back. I'll

call in a few days when we're ready for you."

Giving Tee a pound, he said, "Aiight fam, be easy."

Tavares contemplated his next move as he drove down 41A and turned into New Providence. Already knowing he wouldn't receive a warm reception, he was just hoping to get his foot in the door to explain his side of the story. Turning onto Chapel St., he parked in front of the Abundant Life Outreach Center, then walked around to Lashay's house and knocked on the door. Glancing at his watch, which showed half past one, he knew she was home and probably still in her pajamas barely awake from the long night hours she kept.

After knocking harder, he heard a voice call out, "Hold up, I'm coming." As soon as the door swung open and Lashay laid eyes on Tavares, she tried to slam it shut in his face, but he slid his foot through the opening. Looking at him with contempt she said, "What the hell are you doing here?"

"I need to talk to you about something."

"I ain't got no convo for you deadbeat!" she spat.

"I guess I deserved that, but if you would give me just 30 minutes to explain, you might see things differently."

Hearing the sincerity in his voice and picking up on his determination that he wasn't leaving until he got his point across, she opened the door and said, "You got 15 minutes."

After seating him on the living room sofa while she sat across from him on the ottoman, paying minimal attention to what she thought would be a lame excuse for how he openly dissed Ariana.

As Tavares explained his true motives in pushing her away to protect her and their unborn child from Dee's wrath, she began to listen intently.

"Look, I love Ariana and want nothing more than for us to be a family. As long as Dee is free on the streets, his vindictive nature won't allow this beef to die until it destroys one of us."

"What happened between y'all to make him like that?"

"If I went into all that I would exceed my 15 minute time limit," he joked.

"I guess I can give you an extension."

"To make a long story short, we were once business partners. Our employer favored me more, so when he chose to down size and redirect his business scope, he chose me and my crew to oversee things... to add insult to his pride, ever since we were in school, he's had his eye on Ariana. During that time we knew of each other, but I never approached her because Dee was always talking about wifing her up. Then after getting rezoned from Northeast to Kenwood, I figured our paths wouldn't cross too often, but as fate may have it, the three of us got put in Alternative School around the same time."

"Yeah, I remember that she had got dimmed out for bringing a blade to school and they searched her locker," she interrupted.

"Dee thought with us stuck in a class together, he was guaranteed to win her over. Day after day she did converse with him, but she shot down his advances. One day after lunch, she told me her mom wasn't gonna be able to pick her up and with it raining cats and dogs she didn't want to wait at the bus stop for the CTS. While I was driving her home we got to rappin' and that's how it happened. From then on we were inseparable and Dee hated me for it."

"So all this animosity is over her?" she said, shocked. "I thought real niggas ain't beef over females?"

"You may have just answered your own question... Anyhow in his twisted mind I have always got what he felt should have been his, so he's made it his personal mission to make my life miserable by attacking those around me."

199

"I see it all now. Why didn't you explain it like that to Ariana?"

"You know how she is, especially after y'all's ill-advised plan where y'all jumped Quanetta and Sasha while she was 3 months pregnant. Do you really think she would have backed down and not have insisted on being involved in the big payback?"

"Sounds like you may be cooking something up for Dee."

"It's gonna require a lot of discretion, and I'm gonna need your assistance."

"Count me in." She was more than willing to put in work.

Chapter 17

Over the course of a few weeks, Ariana and Brandon began to grow close. He seemed to be just what she needed to take her mind off of Tee.

After several movie and dinner dates, most of Ariana's defenses were down. He seemed to be the perfect listener as she described the good and bad times with Tee. By now those seemed to be an all too distant memory. She found herself looking forward to seeing where this would go with Brandon.

"So what do you wanna get into?" he asked, as they pulled out of Applebee's parking lot.

"I was kind of hoping that you would take me back to your place," she said.

"Are you sure?" he asked, while inwardly he had been waiting for her to come to terms with her past relationship and move forward.

"Yes," she replied with a slight chuckle.

"And what are you laughing about lil miss giggles?"

"Oh, nothing really... I was just having a nigga moment."

"Girl, you know you don't know nothing about that," he joked.

"If you say so. What I do know is that you got a set of the most gorgeous pussy eating lips I've ever seen."

"Dang that is some nigga ish right there. I didn't even know y'all paid attention to lips like that."

"What's good enough for the goose is good enough for the gander right? I hope you ain't selfish with those Missy Elliot lips."

"I wouldn't call it selfish, more like reserved."

"As long as you reserve some time with me, I'm kosher."

"Okay, now I see what it's like to be hit on as a woman and I must admit I feel kinda cheap, but I like it at the same time."

"Good, cuz it's been almost two months since I got some and I'm horny enough to take it right here at this stop light."

"A real nigga wouldn't talk about it, he would just be about it," he taunted.

Taking the challenge head on, she unzipped his pants and engulfed his manhood before the air could even get to it.

"Shhhhooooot!" Brandon gasped, as his foot absorbed the shock and slid off the break too early.

"Let me know if you can't take the heat because I refuse to be in an accident stuck in this position on the news," she said playfully as her tongue slid up and down his enlarging shaft.

"Don't worry ma, I got this," he growled while allowing his right hand to glide up her spine to the back of her head…

After arriving at his apartment, Brandon began to give Ariana a brief tour of the place, before returning to the living room adjoined to the kitchen and dining room.

"Now if I can get you to have a seat here," Brandon said, motioning to the swivel barstool near the high countertop.

Prior to exiting the room Brandon turned off all the lights with the exception of the dim light above the kitchen sink, then disappeared into his bedroom. Returning moments later with a computer chair, he placed it in front of Ariana.

"What do you have up your sleeves?" she questioned.

"Just a little roll play. Now sit back, relax, and pretend I'm Missy Elliot and you're the spokeswoman for lesbians everywhere," he said, lowering his chair as he licked his lips LL Cool J style then slid up her flowered sun dress and eased down her panties.

Beginning with her left inner thigh he planted damp kisses until his flickering tongue reached her moist lips. Anticipating the euphoric sensation her muscles began to tense up.

Sensing her inner yearning building with each lick, he continued his teasing with trails of kisses along her right inner thigh while his thumb tickled her clit. Gripping the back of her stool as she anticipated his return she let out a low sigh followed by an orgasmic moan as his double jointed thumb snaked its way into her opening performing the wave while his tongue concentrated on pleasing her clit...

Chapter 18

Feeling untouchable, Dee didn't let the news of the massacre that took place at Kebo's spot phase him. Chalking it up as a business loss, he was only concerned with the bottom line. With him secretly being one of Clarksville's biggest drug distributors, he could always find a cutthroat crew to push his product. Dialing his Nashville connect to schedule a re-up to make up for the loss, he was perplexed at getting the message that all three contact numbers were disconnected. It wasn't unusual for one or maybe two numbers to be disconnected at the same time because his connect regularly recycled numbers, but three was completely unheard of.

In his low key home in Ashland City, he cursed a loud. He knew his back up supply was only enough to last a few days with the 1st of the month only two days away. Getting dressed, he grabbed his keys and hit I-24 to coordinate a re-up face to face.

{{{{{{{{{{{{{{{{{{{{}}}}}}}}}}}}}}}}}}}}

Courtney escorted Dee up the stairs and seated him in the private lobby and offered him a drink, which he declined. She glanced at Funk, the bodyguard and nodded before saying,

"Mr. Blanco will be with you in a moment."

After nearly 45 minutes, it was obvious that Dee was getting bored and restless, but as soon as the office doorknob turned he jumped to his feet. Immediately Funk pulled out a Browning 9mm with a silencer and aimed it at him while Courtney patted him down and ran a debugger over him.

"He's clean!" Courtney called out.

"Excuse our hospitality, but we rarely have visitors." Blanc said. "Now that we got that over with... what brings you here?"

"Well, I tried calling in an order, but couldn't get patched through on any of the lines. I had to make sure shop wasn't closed to keep my end from drying up completely." Dee explained.

"Supply and demand, a constant dilemma for business men such as ourselves," he mused.

"All is well on our end. We're just switching things up a bit."

"So how will I be able to contact you?" Dee asked.

Blanc snapped his finger and Courtney passed Dee a cell phone. "I'll get in contact with you. If you receive a call, you will automatically know who it is from." Dee pocketed the phone as Blanc continued, "Don't use it to call anyone and keep it on you at all times, because you will only receive the call one time."

Dee nodded and was escorted to his vehicle by Courtney. Distracted by the change in protocol, Dee never noticed the tail that managed to follow him at a distance through the slow moving Nashville traffic until he reached Exit 19. Turning right on the off ramp, Dee traveled down Maxie Rd., then turned right again on Turnsville Rd. where he followed the winding roads before pulling into his driveway. Meanwhile his tail rode by undetected.

Posing as the transport, Detective Marshall called the re-up burner phone and arranged to meet Dee at the shopping plaza off Exit 11.

The sun was just beginning to set when Dee left to meet the mule. B Durdy knew time wasn't on his side, so he used his expertise in the cat burglar trade to narrow down the locations where Dee would logically keep his safe. Finding it rather quickly, he broke out his equipment and went to work setting up bugging and video devices. Then with gloved hands, he expertly cracked the safe and planted the dirty .38 and half a kilo. He was originally supposed to deposit the full ki, but figured although he was doing this as a favor, compensation was in order. Not to mention the stacks of cash he stuffed in his bag from the safe as an added bonus. After all, where Dee was headed, he wouldn't need that money. Once everything was back in place he slipped out....

{{{{{{{{{{{{{{}}}}}}}}}}}}}}}}

The drop had gone better than expected. Not only did Dee get his package at a reasonable ticket, but the mule had delivered an added bonus in the form of Sharita for the inconvenience in having the process changed at the last minute. Initially, he was caught off guard and suspicious of the whole transaction, until Sharita, (who unbeknown to Dee, was Lashay's cousin) took his mind off the situation by whispering, "I want you to put your big dick in my mouth, my pussy, and in my butt then have you cum all over my face," sensually in his ear.

Dee's eyes lit up as she pulled his hand under her tight skirt and pushed it deep inside her wet pussy then pulled them out and licked his dripping fingers dry. Ordinarily, he would have rented a room, but all Dee could think of was how he was going to beast that pussy.

With lustful desire building they never made it to the bedroom as the door was barely even slammed shut as Sharita began to finish the expert blow job that originated on the car ride home.

Wanting to sample her wetness he bent her over the recliner causing her to moan with delight as he slid his manhood into her void. With him in complete control behind her, his facial expression took on a barbaric look as she moaned, "Come on daddy and take this pussy." Finding his rhythm his skin was slapping against her skin so hard it sounded like he was beating her over and over as she screamed out, "Ahh...oui...oui that's it, right there." As he savagely complied the rocking recliner giving way to his violent thrusts didn't slow them down as it scooted against the wall for support. She began howling and moaning for him to beat her pussy.

Gripping her waist and yanking her back into him as he thrust forward, she pushed her behind backward over and over with her begging for him to go as deep as he could matched by him growling his own obscenities. Dee began to pound her so feverishly that dribbles of spit fell on her backside before he pulled out and grabbed her by her neck as he busted off a massive load all over her face.

After collapsing on the recliner, Sharita smiled and asked Dee where his bathroom was so she could clean up. Still fighting to catch his breath he pointed down the hall for her to figure it out herself. Grabbing her purse she strode down the hallway and found the bathroom on the second door on the right. Once inside she dialed Detective Green's cell phone, which was answered on the first ring. "We're ready," was all she said before hanging up.

The front and rear doors crashed open, taking Dee by surprise, as the FBI and DEA agents rushed inside with high powered weapons pointed at him. Led by Detective Marshall, they moved swiftly throughout the house confiscating drugs and taking pictures. Sharita calmly emerged from the bathroom and walked out of the front door.

{{{{{{{{{{{{{{{{{}}}}}}}}}}}}}}}}}

It's said, "What you sow in the wind can come back 7 times as much in a whirlwind." With that adage holding true, the following morning the Leaf Chronicle would go on to describe how a drug raid resulted in Damian Peeler also known as Dee being charged with conspiracy and possession with intent to distribute over 6 and a half kilos.

After reading the front headline of the event on his back deck, Tee flipped a few pages and intently read over the details. Satisfied with the information contained in the article, he folded up the paper and placed it on the patio table.

With this chapter finally closed, Tee's mind began to revisit the pages filled with love & joy followed by heartache and grief. In spite of the regular money orders and requests sent through Brittany for Ariana to contact him, she never responded.

As his worldly wealth began to deteriorate from riches to rags, he pondered how he was going to maintain his current possessions, take care of his family, and still achieve forward progress with his ambitions.

Considering he had yet to find an employer aside from fast-food and janitorial work willing to hire him, the road ahead seemed congested with obstacles. Thinking back to an Astronomy class he had once taken, Tavares remembered the stressful violent life of stars. With the overwhelming force of gravity maintaining the stars shaped by pushing inwardly on its core in contrast with hydrogen and helium burning as fuel through fusion reactions pushing outwardly providing its warmth and brilliant light. One force without the other would either result in gravity crushing the stars core in a violent explosion or the heat and rays of light would expand out into space until absorbed by another celestial object.

Making the connection of this analogy to his own life, Tavares felt as if his drive and ambition burning at his core was beginning to slow down with the weight of his problems increasing in an attempt to crush him. Feeling as though he was at the point of not being able to bear the weight much longer, he lifted his eyes unto the heavens and asked God to shelter him from the pain…

Chapter 19

By now, although Brandon and Ariana were practically inseparable, she could tell there were aspects of his life that he kept from her. Midway through her third trimester she began to question whether he would be willing to sign the birth certificate and marry her as they had discussed. Even though the love wasn't there as it had been with Tee, for the most part Brandon made her feel safe and secure.

As Tee entered her thoughts, she found herself reminiscing the good old days then quickly dismissed them. She appreciated the money that he sent every month, most of which she deposited into an account for their child. With her making her own money and Brandon being so supportive she really didn't need Tee or his dirty money.

Unaware of the progress that he had made towards getting his life together, Ariana wrote him off as a lost cause. Even the news of the big payback from Lashay couldn't persuade Ariana to consider giving Tee another chance. She just figured a new enemy would soon emerge and the cycle would repeat itself.

"A penny for your thoughts," Brandon said, breaking her out of her trance.

"Oh it's nothing... just ready to have this baby."

"Is that all you're ready for?" he said, licking his lips.

"Am I just a piece of meat for you to devour whenever your stomach starts growling?" she joked.

"Meat? No… more like a tootsie pop that takes over 1,000 licks to get to the center," he said in a husky voice.

"Well if that's the case let me know what the center tastes like," she playfully replied as the duo prepared to engage in some sensuous foreplay…

As the simmering heat from their lovemaking cooled down leaving them in an exhausted state, Brandon fished around the floor near the bed to retrieve his pants.

"And where do you think you're going?" she asked.

"After the way you were throwing them hips back, I gots to fire one up," he replied while pulling a Black and Mild box out of his pocket.

Although she detested tobacco smoke, she was not ready to become unglued from him yet. "You don't have to go, just don't blow it my way."

"Umm… I'm not sure if that's a good idea," he said trying to think of a good excuse. "You know second hand smoke ain't good for babies."

"Despite my disdain for smoke, I am the product of a mother who smoked all through pregnancy. So it's safe to say this one time won't hurt."

Not wanting to ruin the vibe, Brandon sparked up the grape cigarillo.

Almost immediately after the first puff the pungent odor filler her nostrils.

"Wait a minute. I don't even smoke blacks, but I do know enough to know that sure as hell ain't one. There ain't even a tip on that!" she exclaimed.

"Chill ma, it ain't even that crucial," he said in between puffs.

"Why ain't it when you are still active duty and can be drug tested randomly?" she asked.

"I got that all under control. Me and the officer that administers those for our unit go way back. While you talking, I see you eyeing it down like you wanna take a hit."

"It does bring back memories, but I'm pregnant now so that ain't an option."

"Like you said earlier, you turned out fine although your mom smoked through pregnancy. Plus it's medically unproven that weed has any negative side effects on a child's development," he said convincingly.

"Why you sound like Smokey trying to get Craig high on Friday right now," she joked.

"Because it is Friday and right now you're off so you don't got no job, so…" he trailed off while passing the blunt to Ariana. "Come on Craig."

Chuckling slightly, she took the blunt and hit it a few times before passing it back to Brandon.

"See it wasn't that bad was it? Next time around I'm gonna need you to smoke that like you know what you're doing," he said before deeply inhaling the smoke and blowing a donut.

"Whatever. Tricks are for kids. Blow me a shotgun real quick then I'ma show you how to chief."

{{{{{{{{{{{{{{{{{}}}}}}}}}}}}}}}}}}

Life went on with the fall of Dee as several crews emerged to take over his crown.

"Mane who would have thought Dee going down would set the streets ablaze," Vince said during their weekly meeting at Finishing Touches.

216

"Yeah, the body count is steadily increasing from all these young bucks scrambling for a piece of the pie," Donovan added.

"Tell me about it. A handful of them baby gangstas had the nerve to jump stupid with Junior and his Kritikal posse. From the way I heard it went down it's a miracle that the sole survivor barely made it out of the aftermath to tell about it," Roe stated.

"To stay above the melee, I suggest we keep to Tee's advice and utilize his plug with Blanco to supply the biggest crews anonymously," Donovan said as his eyes panned the room until settling on Roe.

"I'm with it. These days being a street legend only makes you a target. Plus I've put in my share of work. It's time to kick back, get paid, and watch this new breed try to get money." Roe replied.

"I just can't figure out why Tee would pass up on this golden opportunity. Instead of having to struggle and ball on a budget, he could be livin' life," Vince questioned.

"With his business savvy mind, it won't be too long before he's back on top. Plus with the way he is gonna go about it, once he gets there, ain't nobody gonna be able to knock him off," Donovan replied… "Now that we are on the same page, me and the wifey got plans," he said, rising to his feet to leave.

"Some things never change," Roe commented as Donovan dapped everyone up. "Mr. Ladies' Man always gotta dip out early to start caking," he joked.

"At least nowadays I'm baking the same cake," Donovan replied before leaving the office.

{{{{{{{{{{{{{{{{}}}}}}}}}}}}}}}}

At long last the van pulled into the Madison St. Shopping plaza and parked in front of Washington Inventory.

Although the pay wasn't great and the hours were long, Tavares was able to pay his bills and still invest a little here and there in his company.

The advantage of working for WIS was that he was able to travel all over Tennessee and surrounding states inventorying stores for free. On breaks and after completing his inventory quota, he would sell books, CDs, and pass out flyers to prospective customers.

As the months went by, his side hustle was able to sustain itself and still generate a small profit. The only downside was that WIS was seasonal. The numbers of stores requesting their services were slowly declining along with the hours for the employees.

Feeling the pinch now, Tavares found himself having to dip into his side hustle profits just to maintain.

The allure of tapping into the drug trade became all the more tempting. HPC even offered him royalties off the top for plugging them in. Wanting to steer clear of going backwards, Tee declined.

As Tee considered his options, he remembered his last discussion with Donovan where he heard about Naomi transferring from operations to Human Resources at Convergys. Going out on a limb, he dialed up Donovan's number.

"Life Living," Donovan greeted.

"Living Life," Tee responded.

"How's the straight and narrow working for ya?"

"Mane, it's a lot harder than I thought it would be. I got to give them square bodies' credit for surviving and succeeding at this life style."

"I know you are trying to make it on your own, but you already know the camp has got your back."

"That's actually why I called. I need a favor."

"I got you fam, what's good?"

"This gig with WIS just ain't cutting it anymore mane. Do you think Naomi might be able to pull some strings and get me on at Convergys?" Tee asked.

"It's possible. Let me talk it over with her first then I'll get back with you."

"Aite. Good lookin' out fam, Life Living."

"Living Life," Donovan replied prior to disconnecting the line.

"Is something wrong baby?" Naomi said sensing something was awry.

"Somewhat… Tee has a situation that he needs your help with."

"Me?" she asked puzzled.

"Yeah, he is real determined to make it back to the top by doing it the right way this time around. Despite him being intelligent and more than qualified for the positions he's been applying for, no one will give him a chance because of his criminal record. Is there any way you can pull some strings to get him on at Convergys?"

"I'm not sure. I can try… Have him apply and leave out all info about his criminal background," she replied.

"Thanks. So, what do you have a taste for?" Donovan asked as they prepared to pull onto Riverside Dr.

"I wanna check that Thai restaurant out down the street."

"Are you gonna have time for the all you can eat buffet? You already know how I get down."

"They'll be alright. The perks of salary are that I don't clock in and out anymore."

"Okay, so what's the difference between Thai and Chinese food? They don't be trying to dish up fried canine and grilled feline do they?"

"You got jokes. They only bring those out for special occasions. Naw, for real though. It's like the difference between Puerto Rican and Mexican food or Up North cooking compared to home southern style. It's a matter of seasoning mainly."

"Okay, as long as it's fully cooked I guess I'm good. Seeing as though you're on your own program do we have time for dessert after this?" Donovan said, looking Naomi over hungrily.

"Maybe, we'll just have to wait and see if your eyes are bigger than your belly."

{{{{{{{{{{{{{{{{{}}}}}}}}}}}}}}}}}}

After being seated and ordering drinks, Donovan let Naomi lead the way to the buffet style spread. Not quite sure what to expect from the imitation China Buffet, he picked out small portions of items he recognized.

Once seated again, he began timidly poking around his plate to the slight annoyance of Naomi.

"Boy didn't your momma tell you not to play with your food? I can assure you that you won't catch bird, swine, or squid flu by eating any of it," she said half playing.

"It's not so much the food, as it is making a tough decision," he replied.

"What's on your mind baby?"

"Now that I'm further removed from the streets and taking online classes at Austin Peay, I'm starting to view things from another perspective," he said in a serious tone as he took a bite of something that kind of resembled fried chicken.

"Are you planning on walking away from that lifestyle?" she asked with optimism in her voice.

"I'm not quite ready to take the high road like Tee, but since I've replaced him as the head of operations, I have a better understanding and appreciation for the time he spent teaching us how to use the game instead of allowing the game to use us."

"Translation?" she probed for clarity.

"Well, without going into too much need to know information, I'm basically transitioning myself to pull strings from the top and stay off the radar so that I can live a normal yet comfortable life without looking over my shoulders."

"So what's new? I've heard you talk of this transition before. I know you're working at it because I'm seeing progress, but it still seems like a long term goal," she said before taking a sip of her pink lemonade and continuing. "What I want to know is how do I fit into the equation?"

"It's funny you ask that because it's a major part of this tough decision I have to make."

"Did something bad happen? Please don't push me away like Tee did Ariana. I want to be there to support you through the good and bad times," Naomi pleaded.

"Baby, it's serious, but it ain't never that crucial," he reassuringly said, placing his hand over hers. "For the most part I've already made up my mind. The difficulty comes into play when deciding how to go about it."

"Go about what? Now you're confusing me with all these riddles."

Undetected, Donovan quickly slipped his free hand in and out of his pocket then lifted Naomi's hand and placed it under his. "Hopefully this clarifies things for you." As a puzzled look came across her face he loosened his grip on his hand being covered by hers and eased it back leaving the item behind. "Naomi... will you marry me?" he asked sincerely while watching her puzzled expression instantly change to one of joyful ecstasy...

Chapter 20

At long last the countdown was coming to a close. Ariana had chosen to induce her labor by 2 weeks to speed things along.

As she reclined on the hospital bed waiting on Brandon and the contractions to appear, thoughts of Tavares intruded her mind.

It had been almost 4 months since they spoke, yet she knew he wouldn't keep her waiting at a time like this. Tee, despite all his ambitions and street loyalty, had always been someone she could count on. Even while he was incarcerated his letters and calls had the ability to uplift her with each word.

"How could he have abandoned me!" she screamed out just as Brandon was entering the room.

"Baby, I'm sorry I'm late. You know I wouldn't abandon you," he responded, thinking that she had been referring to him.

As the scent of weed assaulted her nose, she immediately knew why he had been late. "You sorry excuse for a man!" she shouted. "How could you keep me waiting at a time like this? Just get out. I'll have this baby without you!" she fumed.

"Fine. I've got better things to do than hear you

complain and moan anyway. Plus, I'm leaving for Iraq within 6 weeks and I don't need to be bothered with you or that bastard child!" he retorted.

Instantly reaching for the closest thing to her, she violently launched a cup of ice chips at him as he turned his back to leave. Once the door slammed shut behind him, tears began to stream down her face.

Feeling like a fool for rejecting Tee's reconciliation attempts, Ariana began to sink into a state of depression. Had it not been for the epidural, she would not have had the will to endure the pain and deliver her son.

At 1:07 a.m. on February 10, 2009, Amari Cauthen was born. What should have been a joyous occasion was filled with anguish and despair. As a result, once Amari was cleaned off, Ariana declined holding him. Instead, she opted to have him transferred straight to the nursery while she wallowed in sorrow.

{{{{{{{{{{{{{{{}}}}}}}}}}}}}}}

The next day, Tavares found himself plotting out the quickest way to put his annoying alarm out of its misery. After finally prying his eyes open, he sent the alarm crashing into the trash can.

Despite his reluctance in waking up from a good night slumber, he was thrilled to have a reason to. Naomi had somehow pulled some strings and gotten Tavares hired as a customer service representative. With the five week training behind him, he was ready to prove himself as an asset to the company.

After allowing the steamy water to cascade down his back to aid in waking him up, he stood before his closet to determine what he would wear. Thankfully, he still had some of his old church clothes and a few casual dress outfits so he could adhere to the professional dress code.

As he backed out of his driveway, Tee's ears were greeted by Steve Harvey giving honor and praise to God for blessing him with his radio show. No matter how many times he heard the catch phrase, "Steve Harvey got a radio show," it never got old to him. Having made it through several of life's trials, Tee couldn't help but be grateful for the doors God was starting to open for him. Pulling into the sparsely populated parking lot, Tee again thanked God for the favor He had given him in addition to the natural skills to excel in training as top of his class.

As a result, he was among three agents who got to pick their schedule. If Tee had chosen any of the other later schedules, parking would have been a challenge. As long as he never drove anywhere for lunch, he could avoid the parking headaches and long walks.

Once settled at his cubicle and clocked in, Tee began taking calls practically back to back as if he were a tenured rep who was familiar with the various call types. Occasionally when he came across an issue that he wasn't quite sure how to resolve, he would just use the quick communication chat system for assistance.

Before Tee realized it lunch had arrived just as he was wrapping up the last call. Trina suddenly materialized as he placed his headset on the phone and prepared to get up.

"I know you weren't planning on skipping out on our lunch date tradition?" Trina said, referring to how a few members of their training class always ate lunch together.

"I figured with us all coming in different shifts our lunches weren't gonna be at the same time," Tee replied.

"Does it look like I'm worried about somebody's scheduled adherence? I'm Miss Trina baby, and you betta not forget it!" she declared with the roll of her neck and a snap of her finger like a true diva.

"How could I ever forget when you remind me every day?" he joked.

"Come on boy," she said slapping him playfully on the shoulder. Out of their training class of twenty-two, only sixteen made it through the class with the anticipation that half that number would either be terminated or quit before they had been there six months.

"So what did you bring?" Trina said, eyeing Tee's plastic bag as he bent down to pick it up.

"Turkey Pot Pies," Tee said as he made his way towards the break room.

"I swear you and them dang gon microwavable meals," she said with a disgusted look on her face. "I'm gonna need you to learn how to put in work in the kitchen," she playfully scolded.

"Don't get it twisted. Ya boy can fend for himself. I just be on the grind so hard, that microwaveable fits my schedule."

"I guess," she said, shaking her head. "Ya dog got your back though. I barbecued yesterday and brought in extra meat that is so tender its practically falling off the bone," she proclaimed proudly.

I'll have to be the judge on that one," Tee said, placing his pot pies in the microwave. Once all the food was heated, they found a table to eat their meal.

"So, what ya think Big Daddy?" Trina asked as Tee devoured his portion of the ribs.

"I'm not quite ready to disown momma, but ya definitely did your thing," he said licking his fingers.

"Thank you, thank you," she said taking a bow.

"You know there's something that I've been meaning to get at you about, right?"

Usually Trina was always in a playful and sassy mood. However, her demeanor abruptly grew solemn. "What's up?" Tee asked, while hoping she wasn't going to seriously follow up on all her references in training to them hooking up. While she was cool peoples, Trina just wasn't his type.

"Just so you know, I know all about you," Trina said, leaning in close as if she were worried about others at the table over hearing their convo.

"What do you mean?" Tee inquired.

"Save the innocent act for a natural blond cuz I'm proud of my beautiful black roots," she replied, combing her fingers through her curly hair. "Celeste is my cousin and she already gave me the 411 on you."

"Oh is that right? Well considering I don't know who this Celeste person is, then she can't know too much about me to be giving the real 411," he said, downplaying her.

"While you may not know her like you claim, she definitely knows Naomi. They have been best friends since childhood, so you know after she got attacked up here she told Celeste all about the incident," Trina said in a hushed tone.

"Okay, so what does any of this have to do with me?" Tee asked nonchalantly while wondering how much she actually knew about his past.

"It has more to do with you than you know or are willing to admit. From what I hear, her attack was retaliation from some stuff you and Donovan may have gotten into," she said while studying Tee's face. When he didn't react to her probing attempts, she tried another angle. "You must really be some drug kingpin or the leader of a gang."

Sensing that she was pulling at straws and only probably knew the bare minimum of his ties to the streets, Tee continued to play aloof. "That ain't even my style. You do know that I am a preachers kid right?" he replied, tracing an imaginary halo around his head in the air with his finger.

"Y'all be the worst ones! Just keep in mind you ain't got to lie to kick it," she said, leaning in close and rubbing her hand across his lap.

"I'll keep that in mind," Tee replied uncomfortably. 'Well my break is about up. I'll catch you on the floor," he said rising to his feet.

"Don't be a stranger!" she called out with a beaming smile and a wink as she imagined what his throbbing manhood would feel like engulfed in her juices.

The rest of Tee's day flew by like the first half as he took call after call. Although he appreciated the occasional break in between calls, he preferred the back to back calls which made the day fly by.

{{{{{{{{{{{{{{{{}}}}}}}}}}}}}}}}

Before long, days turned into weeks then weeks into months. In spite of Tavares keeping to himself for the most part, he quickly gained the attention of upper level management who took notice of him meeting all the performance and quality metric standards.

One day as Tavares was returning from lunch he was greeted by a Team Leader he recognized, but had never really spoken to before.

"Excuse me, your name is Tavares right?" the supervisor asked.

Thinking he had possibly done something wrong he hesitantly responded, "Yes sir?"

"I thought so. Just wanted to congratulate you on a job well done. I know you're kind of new and all, but you're rated within the top 10% of all the agents."

"Thanks," Tee replied before walking back to his cubicle to avoid being late for lunch. Before he could take five steps in that direction, another TL by the name of Larry greeted him with a smile.

"Hey man, from what I hear you're on your way," Larry said while patting Tee on the shoulder.

Not quite sure how to take the statement, Tee shrugged and replied, "Hopefully I'm on my way to a specialty team and not out the door."

Realizing Tee was in the dark, "Go ahead and clock under coaching, then find your TL," Larry advised.

Once he clocked in from lunch, Tee set out to find Nikki, his Team Leader, who was not at her desk. After roaming the floor aimlessly, Nikki finally emerged from the smoking area out back. "Hey Nikki, I was told to come see you."

"Have they told you already?" she inquired.

"Y'all are acting real suspect. Who is supposed to be telling me something and what are they supposed to be telling me? I feel like I missed the memo."

"Relax. It's all good," Nikki said with a bubbly smile. "You know about the openings we have for Team Leader right?"

"I think I may have seen an email about it, but to be honest I don't pay much attention to emails. I figure if it's that important you will go over it in a team meeting."

"Well, considering the caliber of the rest of the team, the news would have fallen on deaf ears."

"So, are you suggesting that I apply for the position even though I have only been here for a little over three months?" Tee asked.

"More like telling you that's what you need to be doing. Since you've been on my team I have never had to coach you directly on anything, yet you still continue to meet and exceed all the stats requirements. They are taking applications in the break room. Go ahead and apply. I've got a good feeling about it," she said with a wink then left to join her colleagues in the TL area.

Apprehensively, Tee walked into the breakroom and approached the TL recruiting table to receive his application packet. Although the idea of being promoted and getting paid more appealed to him, Tavares was more concerned with remaining low key. In the back of his mind was the concern of them running a background check for the new position then firing him for lying on his application. Not sure what to do he returned to the phone and waited until his last break to go to HR and talk to Naomi.

As Tavares prepared to swipe his badge and enter HR he realized he didn't even know Naomi's last name. After she got him hired, he made sure he kept his distance from her and HR just to be on the safe side.

Opening the door he was immediately greeted by the receptionist. "How can we assist you today?"

"I was wondering if Miss Naomi is available." Tee asked while scanning the room for her.

"I believe she is finishing up with an interview," she replied, just as Naomi was escorting the applicant out of her office and to the door. "Oh, there she is. Naomi this gentleman needs to see you if you have a moment."

"Come on back," she said to Tee. As they got settled in her office she asked, "So what can I do for you?"

"I just wanted to get your professional opinion as to whether or not I should apply for the Team Leader position," Tee stated.

Taking a moment to ponder it, she weighed the probability of them running another background check on Tavares, she replied, "I think with your prior management experience and work ethic you would be a tremendous asset to the company as a manager. Feel free to use me as a reference and let me know if you would need any assistance with your resume."

"Thank you. I really appreciate you going out of your way for me:"

"Think nothing of it. I have an open door policy. Anytime you need something or have a question, feel free to swing by," she said extending her hand.

"I'll be sure to keep that in mind," Tee replied as he shook hers and rose to his feet to leave.

Chapter 21

"Dang, is this really what my life has boiled down to?" Ariana pondered as she attempted to peer into her own soul through the mirror in her bathroom.

Over the past few months, Ariana found herself sinking further into depression to the point where weed began to fail her in escaping her reality. Needing something stronger to pick her up from the ashes of despair she began rummaging through her purse to retrieve her new best friend.

After quickly snorting a line and a half she went into the living room to see what Amari was wailing about.

"Shut up with all that crying. That's all you do is cry, cry, cry. I'm sick of it!" she shouted as she prepared him a bottle. Although deep down inside she loved her son, Ariana allowed her circumstances and emotions to overwhelm her to the point of being unable to love herself. With the addition of cocaine to her daily diet clouding her judgment, Ariana soon found herself jobless. As Ariana awaited government assistance to kick in, she began dipping into the funds set aside for Amari to keep them afloat and supplement her new found habit.

Outside of the occasional calls from Brittany or Lashay, Ariana felt completely isolated and abandoned. Her aunt had long since disowned her after discovering her drug use and Tee, other than sending her money orders, had given up on opening lines of communication. "To hell with him!" Ariana exclaimed at the mere thought of Tavares. "And there you go whining again with your stankin' tail," she said, holding her nose as she prepared to change him.

Later that afternoon, Ariana found herself in need of some tranquility. While Amari slept, she began to rummage through the house in search of her stash only to discover she was out.

"Dangit!" she sighed in frustration. "When I finally get him to sleep to enjoy my buzz, I wind up being out. I swear if it's not one thing it's another," she complained while digging out her self-made aluminum foil pipe from her panty drawer. Although she preferred powder to weed, she kept some in reserve for hard times like this.

After packing the pipe, Ariana sat back in her reclining chair and began to self-medicate. With each puff lifting her spirits, allowing her to escape reality, Ariana drifted into a blissful state.

"What am I going to do with you?" Tavares said shaking his head at Ariana caked in mud.

"Love me forever?" she replied innocently with a slight chuckle as they entered the hotel room at the Winner's Circle.

"Well they say you can't choose the ones you love so I guess I'm stuck," he said playfully.

"I got your stuck alright," Ariana said while giving him a muddy embrace.

"Thanks. Just when I thought I couldn't get any more mud on me."

"It's your fault," she said, backing away and peeling the rest of her clothes off. "You're the one who chose that spot," she continued, referring to Tee getting the car stuck in the mud that covered the tires resulting in them having to get out and dig a path with their hands.

"Oh, is that so? If I remember right, you were the one wanting to be spontaneous with some exhibitionism and rushing me to find a spot," he countered. "Plus, one advantage to our mud wrestling adventure is round two as I scrub those sensual curves clean in the shower," he said, pulling her into his body with one arm while using his other hand to turn the shower on...

The baby's sudden cries for attention signified an abrupt halt to her tranquil state. "You know what Tee…" she said through clinched teeth as she peered down at her son. "Seeing as though you wanna play the role of Mr. Clean, I'm gonna let you get your hands dirty, too," she continued as she began to change a very stinky pamper.

{{{{{{{{{{{{{{{{{}}}}}}}}}}}}}}}}}

Back in Clarksville, Roe held court on the back patio of his Raleigh Drive town house.

"So you see this game is more than just who has the lowest ticket on a package so they can buy bigger rims and have the flyest gear," Roe said to his 3 top lieutenants. They just returned from a field trip to a handful of Roe's personal and business assets.

"You make it all sound so simple. Without any real credit or jobs, who is really gonna lend us the money to buy some property without us putting up so much cash that we draw attention to ourselves?" Major asked.

"Glad to see your instincts are still intact. Now what I'm going to share with you will go against the 'don't trust anyone, but be loyal to those that are loyal to you' doctrine that I've been preaching," Roe replied, making eye contact with each lieutenant. "The reason I have chosen you three for this knowledge session is because of the potential I see in each of you to perform as one unit. Each of you has demonstrated several strengths and a few weaknesses that complement one another. Coupled with your ability to work efficiently and squash minor beefs between factions, I can see y'all running things like the modern day HPC."

"Those are real big shoes to fill that will definitely take time," Eric said.

"So what do you think is holding y'all back?" Roe asked.

"Just these half breed rival crews out there that can easily be squashed if we pull our resources together. I know I got some hard hitters on deck ready to reach out to these boys in a critical way," Rob said with vigor.

Roe chuckled to himself at the similarities he saw in Rob and himself around that age before replying, "You're partially correct that you all need to pull your resources together, but not to start wars. There will be plenty of opportunities for y'all to gang up on other crews. Just keep in mind that for every action there is a reaction of sorts that you may not see or feel until years later.

"So what type of collaboration are you suggesting?" Eric asked.

"In due time grasshopper," Roe joked. "On the real though, that is a lesson that Donovan will have to break down. In the meanwhile, I suggest the three of you work towards functioning as one unit with each other's best interest at heart."

"Awww, is the legendary cold hearted killer going warm and mushy on us?" Rob playfully taunted.

"Never that. Through the years I've grown a little wiser and understand the importance of brotherhood,"

241

Roe replied, directing them back into the condo.

"Aite, so when are we gonna be able to chop it up with Donovan? You know he's practically married now and his old lady keeps him on lock down so much the homies don't get to kick it much with him these days," Major questioned.

"Yeah, he's wifed up, but that ain't really why he been out of sight lately. I'll let him fill y'all in on all that. Just keep in mind, with any lesson taught there will be tests that follow," Roe responded, making eye contact again with each one. "Over the next few months your progress as a team will be evaluated, and based on your collaboration, will determine when you're ready for the next level."

With that being said, the crew exited the condo and piled into Roe's expedition. As Roe navigated through Clarksville in silence back to the detail shop where the trio left their cars, his mind traveled back and forth from the days HPC first formed to the present. Images of the grit and the grime to the glamour and glory from their rise to the top brought on a sense of pride and accomplishment. But what is true greatness if it dies without an heir.

As Roe scanned the faces of his lieutenants through the rearview mirror, he pondered whether they had the drive and chemistry to be heirs to the HPC throne.

{{{{{{{{{{{{{{{{}}}}}}}}}}}}}}}}

Meanwhile, life went on, business as usual for Tavares. Two months after applying for the Team Leader position he hadn't heard anything from it. Instead, he was recruited to join the Transition Team to train newly hired agents, then was placed on a team that handled escalated calls.

Upon entering his vehicle and starting it up, he was yet again greeted by Steve Harvey's praise to the Almighty God for all His blessings that had been bestowed on him. After introducing the baddest morning crew in radio, Steve began reading one of the strawberry letters addressing yesterday's 30 seconds email blast concerning fathers stepping up to the plate. Of course the single mothers had the phone lines jumping to discuss dead beat dads. In response, a listener had written in detailing his accounts of being a single father and the struggles he went through with the lack of support and consideration that single mothers are given.

Steve initially addressed the letter with humor, as Nephew Tommy and the crew chimed in until Steve took back control and began to speak from the heart. "My friends don't lose hope nor be discouraged. In spite of the trials you go through raising your child, be thankful for the opportunity to go through those trails," Steve said, pausing to collect his thoughts before continuing. "I'm not sure who I'm talking to out there, but I can feel it in my spirit that someone is longing to be able to be involved in their child's life. Be encouraged. God recognizes the sacrifices you have made to walk uprightly and provide for your child from a distance. Just as He brought you through other trials this, too soon shall pass."

As Steve continued to provide words of encouragement, Tavares could feel God speaking to him. Aside from the few photos forwarded to him from Brittany, Tee had yet to lay eyes on his son. Each day Tee felt himself growing closer to God and in turn feeling more at peace about it.

However, as Amari happened to cross his mind, he could feel the void from missing an extension in his life. Once again pulling into the parking lot, Tavares counted it all joy for the many blessings God bestowed upon him then entered the facility.

Like most days, time flew by quickly from back to back phone calls and Tee utilizing his breaks to pass out flyers and network. Over the past few months Tee had coined the nickname "Man of a thousand hustles" because it seemed like every week he was pushing something new from lawn care services to clothing apparel to books & CDs from the authors and music artists he promoted. As his shift was coming to a close, Tee felt his phone vibrating on his hip. With the new cell phone policy in place, Tavares knew better than to even glance at the caller id on the production floor.

After clocking out for the day, he retrieved his phone upon exiting the building and reviewed his call log. "803?" he thought, perplexed at who would be calling him from that area code. He figured it was a music artist who stumbled across his info online.

Opting to deal with it later, he decided to wait until he was in front of his computer before calling the number back.

"It's about time!" a strange yet familiar voice huffed.

"Who is this?" Tavares asked, attempting to place the voice.

"If you ever took time out to check your voicemail before calling back unfamiliar numbers you might have a clue," She said with an attitude.

"Look, I ain't got time for these petty games. From the sound of things this convo isn't about dollars so it doesn't make sense. So if this isn't business related I'm gonna need you to save the drama," He replied annoyed.

"You haven't even seen drama yet. By the way, try this for making sense. Within the next hour I will be at your house to drop off Amari. It's your turn to see what being a single parent all is about," she said then disconnected.

Left in utter disbelief, Tee was flooded with several different emotions ranging from anger to joy to anxiety as he quickly scrambled for the door to hit up Wal-Mart for supplies.

Being new to the whole parenting experience, Tee decided to call a subject matter expert for advice.

"What's up boo?" Tee spoke into the receiver as the call was answered.

"Nothing much favorite son," she said, excited to hear his voice. "What are you up to?" she asked.

"I'm getting ready to be a father!" Tee said matching her excitement.

"What do you mean getting ready to be a father?" she questioned, as her enthusiasm quickly turned into frustration. "I thought I told you if you had another one before marriage that you wouldn't even have to worry about getting a vasectomy because I would neuter you myself," She fumed.

"Dang momma, that was kinda excessive," he replied, not at all surprised by her bluntness. "Besides, as far as I know, I haven't brought any more kids into this world."

"So what's with all this talk about fatherhood?" she asked.

"Ariana just hit me up out of the blue and said she was bringing Amari to me."

"Really? How long do we get to keep him?" she asked with enthusiasm returning to her voice.

"I'm not even sure. All I know is that I have about 30 to 45 minutes before he arrives and I need your advice on what all I should pick up."

"Well, without knowing how long you have him, there's no need to go overboard. I guess you could start with bottles, diaper bags, and a few outfits. How old is he anyway?"

"He's about 5 months," Tee replied.

"Okay, so pick up a few outfits for him size 3 to 6 months. How much does he weigh? Is he on formula or milk? Is he sitting up or lying on his stomach? What about…"

"Hold up mom," Tee interrupted. "I won't know any of that until I lay eyes on him myself. Ariana never kept me posted on his progress."

"I really wish and hope you two work through your differences for the sake of that innocent child. I would start with the formula, milk, pampers, diaper bag, and bottles, then keep me posted as you get more details so I can see about arranging a baby shower."

"Mom, guys don't have baby showers."

"So, did we become an expert at this overnight?" she asked sarcastically. "Because I could have promised I was the experienced one in this field. Now you don't have to stay at the shower long, but you will be there long enough to tell everyone thank you."

"Yes ma'am," Tee conceded, knowing any way other than her way was a lost cause on this issue.

"That's more like it. Love you."

"Love you, too," he said as the line disconnected.

Tavares found himself anxiously waiting as 1 hour turned into 3 hours. After the tongue lashing he had received for calling an hour ago, Tee decided against calling again and instead chose to work on his websites. Initially, building websites was a daunting and frustrating task that gradually, with experience, became a form of creative expression that he found relaxing. The extra money from building sites for churches, small businesses, and other entrepreneurs in the entertainment industry added to the appeal.

As Tee was finishing some maintenance on leaporg.net the doorbell rang. Taking a deep breath, Tavares rose from his desk chair and began to walk up the first flight of stairs when the doorbell rang again. Just as he reached the landing and began to turn the doorknob, his phone went off. Knowing it was probably Ariana being impatient, he proceeded to open the door.

"Took you long enough," Ariana griped as she passed him the sleeping baby. "I hope you went out and bought some baby food. Amari should be hungry and this can of formula is all I have left," she said, handing him the can.

"So how long do I get to keep him?" Tee asked.

"I'll get back to you on that," she replied with a smirk, then turned to leave.

Tavares started to call after her until he felt Amari beginning to stir in his arms. As his light brown eyes fluttered open, nothing else seemed to matter as they locked onto Tee. In that moment Tavares knew that no matter the cost, he would be there for his son. The moment became all the more priceless as the baby smiled and reached out with both arms to be held tightly. Indeed, Tavares knew he had found his Reason.

City Councilman Richard Garrett has gained extensive business knowledge and negotiating skills as the Executive Director of the LEAP Organization. LEAP provides youth development services. As a licensed realtor for Keller Williams Realty, he is known for his tenacity, perseverance, honesty, and fairness. A proud APSU alum, Richard graduated with Honors with a Bachelors in Public Management.

Richard is a former active duty Marine, father of 4, and a husband with strong ties to the community. He is a graduate of Leadership Clarksville and Leadership CMCSS and is a member of Clarksville Rotary, Clarksville Area Ministerial Association, Chamber of Commerce, Clarksville Association of Realtors Public Relations & Charity Relations Committees, and Clarksville Community Partners Group.

In his spare time, Richard is also the CEO of Liberated Publishing, Inc., which he started in March of 2007 after publishing his first novel "Sensual Delights Fantasies of a Poet." His 2nd novel "Reality Check" was published in 2010.

Liberated Publishing, Inc.
1860 Wilma Rudolph Blvd
Clarksville, TN 37040
info@liberatedpublishing.com
931-378-0500

www.LiberatedPublishing.com

Made in United States
Orlando, FL
09 December 2024

55254571R00141